Red Wine Gossips

Red Wine Gossips

Sunainaa Sindhwanii

PAPER TOWNS
PUBLISHERS

PAPER TOWNS
PUBLISHERS

First published by 2025

Papertowns Publishers
72, Vishwanath Dham Colony,
Niwaru Road, Jhotwara,
Jaipur, 302012

Red Wine Gossips

ISBN Print Book – 978-93-6185-570-2

For details or queries, visit: www.sunainasindhwani.com

Cover designed by: Ruhii Sindhwanii

Printed in India

Acknowledgement

WHEN I BEGAN WRITING *RED WINE GOSSIPS*, LIFE changed forever. I lost my father - my eternal source of love and light. The silence he left behind was unbearable, until my dear friend **Jacqueline Jindal** said, *"Show your love for your dad through this book."* That single line became my strength. On his birthday, **March 13th**, I shared the first glimpse of this book - and every word since has been a way of keeping him close.

Along this journey, I met extraordinary women whose stories of courage, grace, and resilience became the soul of *Red Wine Gossips*. Each one reminded me that womanhood is not defined by struggle, but by the quiet power to rise again.

To my **mother**, for showing me and my **sister**, **Geetu** what true strength looks like.

To my **husband**, **Vinay Sindhwani** for his constant support.

To my **son, Gottam Hari Sindhwani**, my gentle reminder to breathe - thank you for grounding me, for believing in me, and for knowing exactly when I need to slow down.

To my **daughter** and co -author **Ruhii Sindhwani**, whose depth and emotional intelligence at just 18 continues to amaze me. Thank you for sharing your insight, your stories, and your soul. From *The Purple Couch* to *Red Wine Gossips* - and now your podcast *@hititoff.official2023* celebrating young entrepreneurs - you never stop inspiring me.

To Mr. Mubarak Sandhu for his support.

To **Papertown Publishers**, and everyone who helped this book take shape.

And to **Durga Maa**, for guiding my heart and holding my hand through it all.

This book is my prayer of love - for every woman who found her strength in silence, and for you, **Papa**, who lives in every story, every emotion and every heartbeat of *Red Wine Gossips*.

Tales

ECHOES OF COURAGE

Divine Intervention

On a bright sunlit afternoon, Tina sat in her living room as she scrolled mindlessly through her phone. It was supposed to be just another lazy Saturday, the kids at their grandparents', Avinash at his weekend golf game. But something felt different today - an inexplicable heaviness sat in her chest, like the air before a thunderstorm.

Her thumb moved mechanically across the screen, past photographs of perfect lives and curated happiness, when suddenly her WhatsApp erupted. Message after message flooded in, the notification sound becoming a rapid -fire assault on her senses. The sender showed no name, just a number she didn't recognize.

Tina's breath caught as she watched the flood of images downloading - blurry at first, pixelated thumbnails that refused to focus. Her finger hesitated over the profile picture of the unknown sender. One tap. That's all it took for her carefully reconstructed world to begin its descent into chaos.

The face staring back at her was one she'd hoped never to see again. Timsy, Ankit's wife. The woman whose life had unknowingly shattered a decade ago when she'd fallen for a man who'd hidden his marriage like a shameful secret. The woman who had every right to hate her.

"No, no, no," Tina whispered, her voice barely audible in the empty house. Her hands trembled as she opened the first image, and the phone slipped from her fingers like water, clattering onto the marble floor.

The images were of her. Private moments from another lifetime, captured without her knowledge. Messages she'd sent in the naive bloom of what she'd thought was love. Every word, every photograph a testament to her foolishness, her trust betrayed not once but twice - first when Ankit had hidden his marriage, and now, twenty years later, when these ghosts returned to haunt her.

Tears carved hot trails down her cheeks as she scrambled for the phone, her fingers fumbling with the de Vice. Avinash. Oh God, what if Timsy had sent these to Avinash too? Her marriage, the life they'd built together after so much struggle, the trust they'd carefully cultivated - all of it hung by a thread.

She dialled his number, each ring stretching into eternity. When he finally answered, his voice was clipped, distant. "I'm in a meeting, Tina."

"Avinash, please, I need to..."

"Later." The line went dead.

The coldness in his voice sent ice through her veins. He knew. Somehow, she was certain he knew.

With shaking fingers, she called Priya, her best friend since college, the one person who knew every scar on her heart. "She found them, Priya. Pictures I didn't even know existed. Messages from twenty years ago. She's sent them to me, and I think... I think she's sent them to Avinash too."

"Breathe, Tina. Just breathe," Priya's voice was steady, a lighthouse in Tina's storm. "Avinash loves you. He knows who you are now, not who you were then. Whatever happens, we'll face it together."

But Tina's instincts, honed by years of learning to read the subtle shifts in her husband's moods, told her this was different. She opened the folder again, forcing herself to look at each image, each message. How had Ankit saved these? Why had he kept them? The violation felt fresh, as if he'd reached across the years to wound her again.

The hours until Avinash returned stretched like pulled taffy. Tina paced the living room, straightened cushions that didn't need straightening, wiped counters that already gleamed. When she heard his car in the driveway, her heart hammered against her ribs.

He walked in looking haggard, his usually pristine shirt wrinkled, his tie askew. Their eyes met across the room, and in that moment, Tina saw everything - his hurt, his confusion, his struggle to reconcile the woman he'd married with the images he'd seen.

"Are you okay?" she asked, though the question felt absurd. "You look exhausted."

"Long day," he muttered, heading toward the bathroom. But he'd left his phone on the coffee table - an unusual oversight for a man who treated his de Vice like an extension of his hand.

The phone seemed to pulse with malevolent energy. Tina knew she shouldn't look, but she had to know what he'd seen, what Timsy had told him. She picked it up, entered the passcode - their anniversary date - and there they were. The same images, the same messages, and more. Screenshots of conversations she'd forgotten, moments she'd buried so deep she'd convinced herself they'd never existed.

"So, you've seen them."

Avinash's voice made her jump. He stood in the doorway, water still dripping from his freshly washed face.

"I didn't know he'd taken pictures," Tina said, her voice breaking. "I never knew he'd saved anything. Avinash, that was twenty years ago. Before us, before everything we've built."

"She came to my office." His words fell like stones into still water. "In front of my colleagues, my staff. She threatened you, threatened the children. She said she's going to the women's cell tomorrow, that she'll make sure everyone knows what kind of woman you are."

Tina's legs gave way, and she sank onto the couch. "Why now? After all these years, why is she doing this now?"

Avinash's jaw clenched. "Maybe because she just found out. Maybe because Ankit finally showed his true colors to her too. I don't know, Tina. But I think... I think you should leave India right now. Take the kids, go to your parents' place in Canada for a while, until things settle down."

"Leave?" The word came out as a whisper. "You want me to run away?"

"I want you safe." But he wouldn't meet her eyes, and when he spoke again, the words shattered what remained of her world. "I need some time to think. About us. About everything. I think... I think we need a divorce."

The word hung in the air like a death sentence. Avinash retreated to their bedroom, the door closing with a finality that echoed through the house. Tina sat frozen, her mind struggling to process how quickly her life had unravelled. This morning she'd been a wife, a mother, a woman who'd successfully rebuilt her life. Now she was exposed, abandoned, alone.

But as she sat in the gathering darkness, something shifted inside her. A small flame of indignation that grew with each breath. Why should she run? Why should she hide? She'd made mistakes, yes, but she'd been lied to, manipulated, and now Victimized again. The pictures were taken without her consent, shared without her permission. This wasn't just about her anymore - this was about every woman who'd been shamed for her past, threatened with exposure, forced to live in fear.

Tina stood up, her legs steady now, and walked to her car. Her advocate friend, Meera, answered on the second ring.

"I need to file a complaint," Tina said, her voice stronger than she'd expected. "Against both of them. For defamation, for circulating private images without consent, for threats and harassment."

"Tina, are you sure? These cases can be brutal. They'll ask questions, intimate questions. Your name might become public."

"Let them ask. I'm done being afraid."

The police station at night was a harsh place of fluorescent lights and sceptical faces. The officer taking her complaint looked at her with barely concealed judgment as she explained the situation.

"So, you had an affair with a married man?" he asked, his pen hovering over the paper.

"I was in a relationship with someone who lied about being married," Tina corrected firmly. "And that was twenty years ago. This is about images being circulated without consent, about harassment and threats."

"Why didn't you come earlier? Why wait until night?"

"Because I just found the courage," she replied, meeting his gaze steadily.

The questions continued, each one designed to shame, to make her reconsider. But Tina answered them all, her voice growing stronger with each response. She was claiming her narrative, refusing to be reduced to a mistake from her past.

When she returned home at 2 AM, emotionally drained but oddly energized, she found Avinash waiting in the living room.

"Where were you?" His voice held a note of concern that hadn't been there earlier.

"Filing a complaint. Against both of them."

His eyes widened. "Tina, that's going to make things worse."

"For whom?" she interrupted. "For you? For your reputation? I've been thinking, Avinash. You didn't ask me for my side. You didn't stand by me. Your first instinct was to tell me to leave, to talk about divorce. Maybe that tells me everything I need to know about us."

The next few days blurred together. Timsy's calls and messages continued, each one more Vicious than the last.

Tina documented everything, screenshot every threat. She visited cyber cells, faced more questions, more judgment, but she didn't stop.

Then, unexpectedly, her phone rang. It was Rhea, an old college friend she hadn't spoken to in years, now married to an influential bureaucrat.

"Tina, I heard about what you're going through," Rhea said, and something in her tone made Tina's composure finally crack. She sobbed into the phone, releasing days of pent-up fear and frustration.

"Listen to me," Rhea said firmly. "What's happening to you is wrong. I'm making some calls. This ends now."

Within hours, things began to move. Higher authorities got involved. The cyber cell took her complaint seriously. Avinash, whether motivated by guilt or genuine concern, filed his own complaint about the harassment at his workplace.

Twelve days. That's how long it took. Twelve days of Tina driving herself from one office to another, presenting evidence, standing her ground. Twelve days of sleeping alone while Avinash maintained his distance. Twelve days of finding a strength she never knew she possessed.

When the call came that Ankit and Timsy had been arrested, Tina felt no triumph, only a deep exhaustion. They confessed - Ankit to taking the pictures with a hidden de Vice, Timsy to the harassment. They would serve fourteen days in custody.

The media picked up the story. "Brave Woman Stands Against Cyber Harassment" one headline read. People she'd never met called her courageous. On the other side, Tina felt anything but brave as she sat in her empty living room, the Victory hollow without her family to share it.

That evening, she called her children home from their grandparents' and told them everything. Not the details, but the truth of it. She'd made mistakes. Someone had tried to use those mistakes against her. She'd fought back.

"We're proud of you, Mom," her daughter said, wrapping her arms around Tina. Her son, typically teenage -awkward with affection, joined the embrace.

Avinash watched from the doorway, his expression unreadable. Later, after the children had gone to bed, he sat beside her on the couch, the first time they'd been this close in two weeks.

"I failed you," he said quietly. "When you needed me the most, I thought about myself, my reputation, my ego. I'm sorry."

Tina looked at him, this man she'd loved, still loved despite everything. "I don't know if sorry is enough anymore, Avinash. You showed me who you become when things get difficult. Maybe that's something we both needed to see."

"What are you saying?"

"I'm saying that I'm grateful this happened." The words surprised even her. "Not for the pain or the humiliation, but for what it revealed. For the strength it showed me I had. For the clarity it brought."

She stood up, walking to the window where the first light of dawn was beginning to paint the sky. "You know what I realized? This was divine intervention. Not the crisis itself, but what came after. Every person who helped, every moment I found courage I didn't know I had, every truth that was revealed. God doesn't always intervene by preventing our struggles. Sometimes, He intervenes by showing us we're stronger than we ever imagined."

Avinash remained silent, and Tina continued, "Rhea appearing out of nowhere, the strength to fight when I wanted to run, even you showing your true colors - all of it was divine intervention. I was tested, and I didn't break. I bent, I nearly shattered, but I didn't break."

"So, what happens to us now?" Avinash asked.

Tina turned to face him, really seeing him for perhaps the first time. "I don't know. But whatever happens, I know I'll be okay. That's the real gift in all of this - knowing that I can stand alone if I need to. That my worth isn't determined by my past or by who stands beside me, but by the strength I carry within."

As the sun rose fully, bathing the room in golden light, Tina felt something she hadn't experienced in years - a complete, unshakeable faith in herself. The divine intervention hadn't been a miraculous rescue from her troubles. It had been the discovery that she could rescue herself.

Whatever came next - reconciliation with Avinash, single motherhood, or something entirely unexpected - she would face it with the knowledge that she had walked through fire and emerged not unscathed, but undefeated. And perhaps, in the end, that was the greatest divine intervention of all.

"She laughs, she breaks, she heals - and she lives beyond the Red Wine Gossips."

The Wedding Card

THE MORNING SUN FILTERED THROUGH THE GAUZE CURTAINS of their modest apartment in Mumbai, painting golden stripes across Ria's face as she stirred awake. Beside her, the bed was already empty, but the lingering warmth and the familiar indent in the pillow told her Raghav hadn't been gone long. She could hear him humming in the kitchen - that old Kishore Kumar song he always butchered but sang with such conviction that she'd learned to love his version more than the original.

Five years. Five beautiful, complicated, imperfect years they'd built together in this two-bedroom flat that overlooked a busy street market. No marriage certificate bound them, no sacred fire had been walked around, no vermillion marked her forehead - but what they had felt more real than any ceremony could make it.

"Coffee's ready, lazy bones!" Raghav called out, and she smiled, wrapping herself in his oversized shirt from the night before.

In the kitchen, he stood with his back to her, his shoulders tense despite the casual tone. When he turned, she noticed the slight tremor in his hands as he passed her the mug - exactly how she liked it, two sugars, just a splash of milk.

"I need to go home for a few days," he said, not meeting her eyes. "Ruhani's getting married."

Ruhani - his younger sister whose photograph he carried in his wallet like a talisman. Ria had seen it countless times - a young woman with Raghav's same deep -set eyes and stubborn chin, always smiling as if she knew a secret the world didn't.

"That's wonderful!" Ria exclaimed, though something cold settled in her stomach. "When do we leave?"

"Actually..." Raghav rubbed the back of his neck, that nervous habit she knew so well. "It's very traditional, you know how my family is. They don't even know about. us. It would create unnecessary drama at Ruhani's wedding."

The words stung, but Ria swallowed them down with her coffee. They'd had this conversation before - about his orthodox family in some remote village in Rajasthan, about waiting for the right time to tell them about their relationship. She'd been patient, understanding. After all, hadn't she hidden their relationship from her own parents!

"How long?" she asked quietly.

"Just a week. Maybe ten days." He pulled her into his arms, and she let herself melt against his chest, breathing in the scent of his cologne mixed with the Old Spice soap he'd used since college. "I'll miss you every second."

"I need fifteen thousand for the wedding preparations," he added, almost as an afterthought. "You know how it is - the brother has to contribute."

Ria nodded. It wasn't the first time. Over the years, there had been many such requests - Ruhani's college fees, Ruhani's medical emergency, Ruhani's computer courses. Raghav worked at the same startup as her, but somehow his money always seemed to disappear into family obligations. She'd never minded. That's what you do when you love someone - you become their safety net, their support system.

The morning he left, Ria helped him pack. She folded his clothes with the military precision he liked, tucked in a packet of his favourite cookies, and slipped a note into his shirt pocket: "Come back to me soon. This home is just walls without you."

He kissed her at the door - deeply, desperately, as if trying to memorize the taste of her lips. "I love you, Ria. More than you'll ever know."

Those were the last words he ever spoke to her.

The first week passed in a blur of work and waiting. Ria would catch herself checking her phone every few minutes, but Raghav had warned her about poor network coverage in his village. By the tenth day, worry began creeping in like moisture during monsoon season - slow, invasive, impossible to ignore.

She called their boss, Arjun, who had been their friend since before they'd become a couple. "Have you heard from Raghav? He was supposed to be back by now."

Arjun's confusion was genuine. "Raghav? He has gone for six months leave, Ria what happened, I can see you are missing him terribly because its only two months back, Raghav has gone. Six months, Ria was shocked as Raghav told her three months only .Arjun could easily make out that something was not right there but he chose to be silent that moment.

The room spun. Ria gripped the edge of her desk, knuckles white."

The silence on the other end was deafening.

Days turned into weeks. Weeks into months. She couldn't file a formal missing report because that could lead back to his home where their relation wasn't informed. She had to suppress all her instinctive thoughts for the time being. It was as if Raghav had simply evaporated, leaving behind only the ghost of his presence in every corner of their apartment.

The bed they'd shared became an ocean of cold sheets. The kitchen where he'd made her coffee every morning echoed with silence. His favourite mug sat untouched on the shelf, gathering dust like abandoned hope. She kept paying rent for both of them, kept his clothes in the closet, his toothbrush by the sink - as if maintaining these rituals could somehow summon him back.

Six months in, she'd stopped eating properly. The weight fell off her frame like autumn leaves. Dark circles became permanent residents under her eyes. She'd wake up at 3 AM, certain she'd heard his key in the lock, only to find the emptiness mocking her.

It was Nitika, her best friend since school days, who finally staged an intervention after a year had passed.

"Ria, you have to let go," Nitika said gently, holding her friend's frighteningly thin hands. "This apartment... it's become a tomb. You're haunting your own life."

"What if he comes back?" Ria whispered, her voice hoarse from crying. "What if he comes back and I'm not here?"

"Then he'll find you," Nitika said firmly. "But you can't keep living like this. You're disappearing, and not in the way he did - you're fading away bit by bit."

It took another month, but finally, Ria agreed to move. Arjun, who had been quietly supporting her through the ordeal, helped them shift her things to a new place closer to the office. He never asked for anything in return, never pressed his advantage, just remained a steady, comforting presence in her chaos.

Fourteen months after Raghav's disappearance, Ria found herself standing outside their old apartment. The new tenants were away, and the landlord had asked her to clear out some mail that kept arriving in her name. The familiar climb up three floors left her breathless - not from exertion, but from the weight of memories.

The mailbox was stuffed with promotional flyers and bills. She sorted through them mechanically until her fingers found an envelope that felt different - thicker, more formal. It was covered in dust and had been there for months, wedged at the back of the box.

She wiped it clean with trembling fingers. The moment the names became visible through her tears, her legs gave way.

RAGHAV WEDS RUHANI

The wedding invitation was elaborate - gold embossing on cream paper, adorned with images of Lord Ganesha. The date was two weeks after he'd left. The venue was in Bangalore, not some remote village in Rajasthan. And the bride's photo...

It was the same girl, his supposed sister.

The woman in the wallet photograph smiled up at her from the wedding card, dressed in bridal finery, her eyes no longer holding secrets but revealing the biggest deception of all. Ruhani. Not his sister.. His bride.

Nitika found her an hour later, still on the floor, clutching the card like evidence of a murder - which, in a way, it was. The murder of trust, of five years, of a future she'd painted in her mind with such vivid colors.

"I knew something was wrong," Nitika said after reading the invitation, her voice shaking with rage. "All that money he took from you, it was never for a sister, was it? It was for her. For their life together."

The pieces fell into place with sickening clarity. The business trips that had increased in frequency. The phone calls he'd taken on the balcony. The way he'd been slowly moving his things out - she'd thought he was decluttering, but he'd been evacuating. The extension of leave, Arjun had mentioned. He'd been planning this for months, maybe years.

"You have to file a case," Nitika insisted. "Financial fraud, emotional manipulation - he can't get away with this."

But Ria surprised her. And herself.

"No," she said, standing up with a strange calm settling over her. "I've already wasted fourteen months mourning someone who never there for me, now, I won't waste another day for the one who invalidated my existence, my emotions."

Ria was so deeply hurt that, it absolutely shifted her emotionally to a more practical and a matured version of herself. Ria threw herself into work with a focus that impressed even Arjun. She started therapy, began eating properly, joined a dance class she'd always wanted to try. Slowly, the color returned to her cheeks, the light to her eyes. Arjun watched this resurrection with quiet admiration. He'd loved her for years - long before Raghav, during Raghav, and now after. But he'd never said a word, respecting her choices, her grief, her healing process. It was Ria who made the first move, six months after finding the wedding card.

"Would you like to have dinner?" she asked him one evening as they worked late. "Not here. Somewhere nice. Like a date."

His smile could have lit up the entire office. They took it slow, building something real on the foundation of friendship and mutual respect. Where Raghav had been storms and passion, Arjun was steady warmth and reliability. He didn't try to make her forget; he helped her remember who she was before the heartbreak. When he proposed eight months later, it wasn't dramatic or elaborate. Just the two of them on her favourite beach in Goa, watching the sunset paint the sky in shades of healing.

"I don't want you to say yes because you're trying to move on," he said, holding out a simple solitaire ring. "I want you to say yes because you want to move forward. With me."

"Yes," she said, and meant it.

Finding Raghav's address was easier than expected. The bank where she'd been transferring money all those years had records. He lived in a middle-class neighborhood in Bangalore, in a house that her money had probably helped furnish. She went alone, despite Nitika and Arjun's protests. This was something she needed to do herself.

When Raghav opened the door, the colour drained from his face as if someone had pulled a plug. He looked older, softer around the middle, with the beginning of grey at his temples. Behind him, she could see a pregnant Ruhani - no longer the slim girl from the photograph.

"Ria..." he breathed, his voice cracking.

She didn't let him speak. With calm precision, she handed him the wedding invitation he'd sent to their old address - whether by accident or cruel design, she'd never know.

"You forgot to include the return gift," she said evenly, then served him with legal papers. "Fraud charges for the eight lakhs you stole from me over five years. My lawyer will be in touch."

His hands shook as he read the documents. Ruhani appeared beside him, her eyes wide with shock as she began to understand who Ria was.

"Oh," Ria added, pulling out another envelope from her purse. "I almost forgot."

She placed her own wedding invitation in his trembling hands. The date was two weeks away. The card read: *Ria weds Arjun*.

"I thought it's only polite to invite you," she said with a smile that didn't reach her eyes. "After all, you showed me what real love isn't. Thanks to you, I now know what it is."

She turned and walked away, her heels clicking confidently on the pavement. Behind her, she could hear Ruhani's voice rising in anger, Raghav's fumbling explanations. But those sounds belonged to another life, one she was finally leaving behind. As her taxi pulled away, Ria felt the last chains of the past fall away. The wedding card had been meant to destroy her. Instead, it had set her free.

Two weeks later, as she walked around the sacred fire with Arjun, she thought she saw a figure at the back of the wedding hall - someone who looked like Raghav. But when she looked again, there was no one there. And it didn't matter anymore.

Some invitations are meant to be declined. Some loves are meant to be survived. And some wedding cards, even the ones that break your heart, can lead you exactly where you need to be.

"She laughs, she breaks, she heals - and she lives beyond the Red Wine Gossips."

Tangled in the Dark

I sat in the dim glow of my bedroom, the only light coming from my phone, which was nearly dead. I could not bring myself to plug it in. I'd been staring at the same message for what felt like hours, my thumb hovering just above the screen.

"Where are you? "Pick up"

His words. Always so heavy. Always so suffocating.

Then another buzz.

"Why aren't you responding? "Are you trying to ignore me BABY?"

My heart skipped. That familiar wave of anxiety crept in like it always did. I did not want to reply. I did not want to explain where I was or why I was silent. But I always did. I always found myself apologizing, even when I had not done anything wrong. I had not been with anyone else, and he was the love of my life which was enough to keep me going. I tossed the phone aside and lay back on my pillow, eyes tracing the cracks in the ceiling. My room was quiet, but my mind was loud buzzing with doubts, frustrations, questions I didn't want to ask aloud. I could feel the weight of everything pressing down on my chest, on my heart, on the parts of me I used to recognize. I had never been one to speak up. Never the one to demand anything -not from him, not from anyone. I was always the one who understood. Who always comprised. He had promised me the world once. He told me I was special. That we were meant to be. And I believed him. And in the beginning, it felt like love. Real love.

But now?

Now, every word from him felt like a knife, every gesture like a chain around my wrist. I could feel myself slipping day by day, argument by argument, subtle jab by subtle jab.

"You're so sensitive."

"You're overreacting."

"I'm just trying to help you."

But it did not help. It was control. It was manipulation. Every time I tried to stand up for myself, to carve out just a little piece of independence, he would twist things. Make me doubt myself. Make me feel like I was the problem.

And I believed that too.

I felt trapped. And I knew it. But still... how could I leave? What if he needed me? What if he changed? He wasn't a bad person, I told myself. Just hurt. Tired. He needed me.

And I loved him?

So how could I leave. I found myself scrolling through my phone, just trying to escape my own thoughts. That is when Jenny's message popped up.

"Hey, I've got a book for you."

The book was *Hamlet*. I'd heard of it, sure. But never read it.

"Sure, I'll pick it up tomorrow," I replied at once, desperately trying to find a way to run away from my thoughts.

When I held the book the next day, it felt heavier than I expected -like it carried something more than just words. *Hamlet* was full of pain, betrayal, and confusion. His world was chaos just like mine. And that famous line - "*To be or not to be...*" -echoed in my head. I had asked myself that same question more times than I cared to admit. Was it better to stay, even if staying was killing me slowly? Or was it better to leave and lose the love of my life? But I wasn't Hamlet. I didn't have his passion, his rage.

No. I was someone quieter.

I was Ophelia.

I was the girl trying to hold it all together, trying to please everyone, trying to love someone who only ever gave me pain in return. Like her, I had been pulled in every direction -by love, by expectation, by silence.

She drowned in it.

And I felt like I was drowning too.

Then another vibration from my phone.

"Are you with someone else?"

The dread returned - sharp but gut-deep. I stared at the message, my thumb hovering just above the screen. Words. Always words. Cold, composed, calculated -meant to twist, meant to bind. Not shouting. Not slamming. Just a perfectly crafted sentence meant to make me feel small. Again. I reached for the book - *Hamlet.* Ophelia, adrift in her madness. Used. Controlled. Discarded.

My heart clenched. I knew her. I was her. At least, I thought I was. But then I looked over at the phone. That tiny screen. That blinking cursor. The stream of messages, love laced with control. Ophelia did not get texts like these. Her oppression was not typed. It wasn't timestamped or archived.

It wasn't screenshots and unsent drafts. It was silent, systemic, inherited. Her leash was obedience. Mine was manipulation masked as care. I turned back to the page. I imagined her there soft, breaking, voiceless. Drowning not just in water, but in expectation. In a world that never asked what she wanted. And for the first time, I did not see myself. Not really. Because I have something she didn't. I have *this*. A phone that pings. A mind that questions. A world that, despite it all, has started to listen. I can choose to speak. To leave. To fight back.

I walked to the mirror. Just stood there. I watched myself breathe. I watched the way I carried tension in my shoulders, the tiredness in my face. But then I noticed something else. A flicker behind my eyes. A question forming.

What if I'm not Ophelia?

What if I don't have to play tragic?

"I'm not her," I whispered. "I don't have to drown in this."

My heartbeat louder now. Not with fear, but with... clarity. No, I wasn't ready to disappear, to run in the night. But I *was* ready to accept what I saw. Ready to accept that love doesn't come with conditions.

Tonight, I won't answer him. Not because I'm afraid. But because for the first time, I understand that silence -*my* silence - can be power. I stood by my window and let the night wrap around me like a possibility. I don't know exactly who I'm becoming.

But I want to find it now.

"She laughs, she breaks, she heals - and she lives beyond the Red Wine Gossips."

WHISPERS OF WISDOM

God's Alarm

THE APPLAUSE ROARED LIKE A TSUNAMI CRASHING INTO a beach. At 24, Jasper had made a phenomenal contribution to the world of literature. She was clad in her grandmother's floral honeymoon dress, which still smelled of roses after all these decades. Today she was sitting amongst the world's most famous writers. It seemed like eternity for the announcer to shuffle to the podium. When he did, the audience again erupted in applause. Jasper got up from her seat in the same manner that a wounded dove might rouse from its nest. Her hands began shaking. There was a lump in her throat. Would she be able to speak? She received the award and thanked everyone present. Then she was asked to share her experiences, which involved rape and recovery from drug addiction. She sighed and started speaking with a trembling voice. Did they all take her for a fool? Did that even matter? She found herself thinking about her abuse and her secret drug taking. Over the years she had surrendered to the fear of her abuser, spending too many nights in the back rooms of fancy night clubs wishing to be well.

The regret of never being rescued followed her around like a stray dog. Now her life seemed to be confined to her bedroom - crying over the way she'd cut her wrists, and hid the scars with tattoos. It was Thursday September 28th, her brother Kevin's birthday. Kevin got shot and killed during the Iraq war. She remembered the soft sound of his voice, and all the times they went swimming together. After all the years, the pain of his loss still felt like a strange sort of crucifixion. An undeserved death. She heard a knock at the door, which shot through her like a thousand volts of electricity. Nobody ever knocked. She got up feeling like a gull that had been out at sea for too long, or a bear that spent too much time in a den. Jasper looked like a skeleton, her skin was wrapped tightly around her joints. She looked up and saw a familiar face. She couldn't believe it. Kevin. She looked at his smiling face, which beamed like the sun through her clouds of depression. Kevin kissed her on the forehead, took her to the living room, and made her comfortable on the couch. He wiped her tears, and assured her that everything was going to be fine. "I have come back for you," he said in his beautiful voice. "To help you with your life. Everyone has a calling in life. Your life has a great purpose." She nodded and kept her head in his lap. She felt love and affection for the first time in years. "Get some rest," Kevin said. "We have somewhere to go tomorrow."

Kevin got up at five in the morning and knocked at her room. He opened the door and sat next to her. Jasper felt his angelic touch on her forehead and rose with a smile on her face. She knew that Kevin was taking her to a special place.

She trusted him, although the mystery of his absence lingered. They arrived 30 minutes later, a lone wooden house in the middle of a great field of wheat. It was like dream. Was she still sleeping? They entered the house and were greeted by a very tall, square jawed man named Doctor Riley, who had several diplomas on his office wall. He was a renowned hypnotherapist and soul-reader. His face was radiant like a sunflower. Was he an angel? Kevin told her to take a session with Doctor Riley. She couldn't say no. Would there ever be an end to the pain? She felt a kind of authenticity and audacity in Doctor Riley. More like a nurse than a doctor. He told her to come inside his office, which was painted with flowers and wild animals.

"How are you feeling Jasper?" said Riley.

"I am okay," said Jasper.

"Good, I'm going to help you today. Will you co -operate with me?"

"I'll try," said Jasper, holding a new hope.

"Great," said the doctor.

"Will you really help me?" said Jasper.

"Yes, of course," said the doctor, who could see the loneliness in her eyes.

"OK, good, now just look at this hanging crystal. Forget everything. Focus."

Jasper looked at the crystal, and gradually closed her eyes.

"Jasper can you hear me?" said the doctor.

"Yes."

"Go back to your childhood. What can you see there?" he asked.

"Mom and Dad are fighting," said Jasper.

"I'm standing in a corner, scared and fearful. Kevin is holding my hand. Dad stormed out of the house. Mom just pulled Kevin's hand from mine, and took him to the room."

"Why didn't she take you with her? Is she your step mom?" asked the doctor.

"No, she is my mom. But she thinks I'm unfortunate because she lost her father the same day I was born. I really felt rejected. I went out to meet my friends. They also made fun of me because I'm quiet dark skinned."

"Ok, tell me about your school and classmates," said the doctor.

"Yes. I studied at Lake Drive School. I really liked going to school. All my teachers were very nice to me," said Jasper.

There was a long pause.

"Why did you stop Jasper?"

"It was Ken. I hated him."

"Why?"

"He touched my private parts in the corner of the school building," said Jasper. "Sometimes he raped me in the bushes next to the playground."

"Didn't you complaint about him?" asked the doctor.

"No, I didn't. I was scared that my mom would hate me for it."

"No, she would have helped you, Jasper."

"I started hating myself because I knew I was not beautiful," she explained.

"Ken told me that he did all this to make me feel good."

"He was an absolute criminal. Did you ever meet him again?" asked the doctor.

"No, never," said Jasper. "I left school."

"Do you still want to punish him?" he asked.

"Yes."

"So Jasper, did you pass high school, too?"

With a cheerful voice she said, "Yes I did. I enjoyed studying with my bestie, Susan. We both had a great time. She was very charming. Every guy wanted to be close to her, but she loved this boy named Alex."

"That's wonderful," said the doctor.

"Susan never gave me a hard time. She was protective of me," said Jasper

"So you really loved being around them?"

"Yes, I did. Until their last date."

Tears started rolling down Jasper's cheeks again.

"What happened Jasper?"

"I am not a good girl. No one loves me. People just use me for pleasure. I am a social misfit. I can't love anyone. Everybody leaves me," she cried.

Riley didn't stop her.

"Are you fine?"

"Yes," responded Jasper.

"Good, can we talk now?"

Jasper nodded.

"Can you please share more about Susan and Alex?"

"We three were very happy together. Alex and I were planning Susan's surprise birthday at Alex's house. We told Susan to come there. I came a little earlier than Susan."

"Great, was Susan happy?"

"No, she was not," Jasper said.

"Sorry, I don't understand."

"I spoiled everything," said Jasper.

"Why do you say that?"

Jasper "But never expressed it, as I didn't want to lose both of them.

That day, Susan couldn't come as her mom was sick. Alex and I were upset. Alex offered me drinks. I wanted to be around him. I almost lost my senses. He was setting up for dinner, when I held him tightly and said I love you. Then he just pushed me back and shouted and asked me to leave. I was lying on road, out of my senses, on a cold winter night. I called Kevin, and he dropped me off at my place, as I was not living with my parents anymore. Kevin was really concerned, but that night he didn't discuss anything. He stayed with me at my place.

"The next morning, Kevin asked about the previous night, but I simply told him to leave. He already knew my anger, so he just left. I went crazy when I realized my mistake. I had deep regret and guilt. What I did was absolutely unethical, and I knew I'd lost my best friends forever. I also hurt Kevin."

Dr Riley said, "Relax Jasper, I do understand your pain, but you're forgetting that you were drunk, and what happened was not in your control. We are just human beings, and we all make mistakes sometimes, which we never expect fromus. You could say sorry to them."

"Yes, I did, but Susan told me to stay away forever," explained Jasper.

"I never saw them again"

"So you left school too?"

"Yes, I joined another high school, where nobody knew me," said Jasper. "Did you study further?" asked the doctor.

"No, I started working part time," Jasper said.

"I was a complete alcoholic by then. I was also shooting up.

Rejection started killing me day and night. I was on a destructive path."

"Destructive? What did you mean by that?" asked the doctor "I was having multiple affairs. I just wanted to be accepted. I got stuck in a chain of broken relationships. Nobody wanted to stay with me for very long. I offered myself to everyone. I felt physically connected, but that was it. Some of the men were jerks, too. They just stayed for my money and my body.

I never said 'no' to anyone, because I didn't want to lose. I was taking more drugs by that time. I lost my job, too. I locked myself behind doors and became aloof."

The doctor said, "Did Kevin or your mom ever visit you? Did they help you? Did you ever go back home?"

"No, I did not want to go back home," said Jasper. "I didn't want to face my mom's rejection. Then Kevin called, and told me to come back home. But I said 'no' to him. One day he called me again, and I just rushed to home. Both my parents had died in a car accident. I was shocked," explained Jasper as more tears streamed down her face.

"Did you go to their funeral?" asked the doctor.

"No, why would I?" said Jasper. "My mom never gave me a chance to say 'I love you'. I wanted her to love me, too. I wanted to cry in her arms." Jasper started to scream.

Dr. Riley was quiet. He didn't stop her from crying. It was an hour now. Tina fell into deep sleep. After four hours, around evening, she opened her eyes slowly. She looked around for Kevin. She got up from the recliner.

"Are you okay," asked the doctor. She remained silent. Doctor Riley called her name again.

"Jasper are you ok?" he asked.

Jasper sat on a chair close to Dr. Riley.

"I am fine," Jasper replied.

Doctor Riley already knew she had been healed by the experience. Jasper looked up. All of a sudden life was beautiful. She knew that happiness something to create.

"Life is not just about carrying a single emotion for a life time," said the doctor. "A deep rejection from childhood can be painful. If you crave acceptance from others, you can forget your identity. You put your existence at stake, just for the sake of approval. Nothing comes from the outside. Peace is an inside game. Self -acceptance is the core of everything. Absolute self -love, and unconditional acceptance start with you. Your mom never rejected you. She was in deep sorrow about her father's loss, and she was not able to cope. She did love you."

Jasper was listening of every single word. No sorrows, No guilt, No rejection. This happened because you finally released your emotional baggage," said Dr. Riley gently. "You let go of the toxic emotions and forgave everyone who hurt you. Jasper, we have to feel the wound to heal it. Protect your peace. I've treated you now let God restore you. Don't let your past steal energy from your beautiful present." Jasper hugged her gratefully and left, a lightness in her chest she hadn't felt in years. But as she stepped into the quiet lobby, a sudden thought struck her where was Kevin?

Beep -Beep -Beep. Suddenly an alarm went off. Jasper rose from her bed.

She immediately stopped the alarm and began looking around anxiously. There was no one. She rushed to the phone and called Army Headquarters. She asked about Kevin. It was unbelievable that Kevin was still dead. He had visited in her sleep. Her eyes caught a glimpse of a wristband on her bed, which said, 'I love you sis'"

She picked it up and remembered that Kevin had given it to her on her sixth birthday. She realized that God had brought Kevin's spirit briefly back into her life. She wasn't alone anymore. Jasper only lived another three months. She, too, died in a car accident. She must have joined Kevin, Doctor Riley, and her parents in heaven, where they spent eternity together.

"She laughs, she breaks, she heals - and she lived beyond the Red Wine Gossips."

The Midnight Dream

THE DARKNESS PRESSED AGAINST THE WINDOWS LIKE A living thing, thick and suffocating in its intensity. It was 2:47 AM when Shona's eyes flew open, her chest heaving as if she'd been running for miles. The sheets were twisted around her legs, damp with perspiration, and her heart hammered against her ribs with such force she thought it might break free. A sob tore from her throat before she could stop it -raw, primal, the kind that comes from a place deeper than conscious thought.

"Gauri?" Her voice cracked as she reached across to the other side of the bed where her daughter sometimes slept when nightmares plagued her. But her trembling fingers found only cool, rumpled sheets and a pillow still bearing the indent of a head long since departed. The emptiness sent fresh waves of panic crashing through her. "Gauri! Gaurav!"

The names ripped from her throat, sharp enough to cut through the peaceful silence of their suburban Canadian home. Within seconds, she heard the thunder of footsteps on the hardwood floor, and then both her children burst through the doorway, their faces masks of alarm in the pale moonlight streaming through the curtains.

Gaurav, tall for his twenty four years with his grandfather's gentle eyes, reached her first. He wrapped his strong arms around her shaking form while fifteen-year-old Gauri scrambled onto the bed, her delicate hands stroking her mother's hair with practiced tenderness. They'd done this before too many times since they moved to Canada, since life had become a series of adjustments and compromises. "Mom, breathe," Gaurav murmured, his voice steady despite the worry etched across his features. He grabbed the water glass from her nightstand, pressing it gently to her lips. "Small sips. That's it."

The water was cool against her parched throat, but it did nothing to wash away the metallic taste of fear. Shona's hands shook so violently that Gaurav had to steady the glass. Over the rim, she caught the look that passed between her children - a silent communication perfected over years of managing their mother's anxiety attacks. But this time, there was something different in their exchange. Something that made her stomach clench with fresh dread.

"What is it?" she gasped, pulling back to search their faces. "What aren't you telling me? Did something happen?"

The speed with which they both replied "No Mom, nothing, all good" only heightened her suspicion. Their voices overlapped in their haste, too quick, too rehearsed. Shona's fingers found Gaurav's collar, pulling him closer as fresh tears spilled down her cheeks.

"Please," she whispered against his shoulder, feeling him stiffen slightly at her touch. "Please tell me your Grandfather is okay."

The silence that followed was deafening. Gauri's hand stilled in her hair, and Gaurav's breathing hitched just slightly, tell that any mother would recognize. Shona pulled back, her dark eyes wild as they searched her son's face.

"I had a dream," she said, the words tumbling out in a rush. "About your grandfather. Oh God, it was so real. So terribly real." Her voice broke on the last word, dissolving into sobs that shook her entire frame. "But I just spoke to him. An hour ago. We talked about his garden, about the mangoes ripening on the tree he planted when I was born. He was laughing. He was fine!" She turned desperately to Gauri, grasping her daughter's small hands. "You talked to him too, didn't you, baby? Tell me you talked to him."

Gauri's eyes, so like her own, filled with tears she was trying desperately to blink away. "Yes, Mama," she whispered, her voice barely audible. "Yes, he's... you need to sleep. Your medication, remember? Sometimes it causes vivid dreams." But even as her daughter spoke, Shona saw the truth written in the tremor of her lips, in the way she couldn't quite meet her mother's gaze. The room began to spin, reality and nightmare blurring at the edges until she couldn't tell where one ended and the other began.

"How can they do it?" The words escaped her in a broken whisper, more to herself than to her children. "How can they just... just..." Gaurav's hand covered hers, warm and solid and real. His wrist bore faint red marks where she'd gripped too tightly, but he didn't pull away. "Mom, tell me about the dream." Shona lifted her gaze to meet his, and in that moment, she saw not her grownup son but the little boy who used to crawl into her bed during thunderstorms, seeking comfort from the only parent who was always there. The role reversal made her heart ache in ways she couldn't articulate.

"I saw him," she whispered, each word feeling like ground glass in her throat. "Papa was... he was on the floor. Not moving. Just lying there in his white kurta, the one I sent him last Diwali. And there was a call, a video call. My cousin Raj, he was crying. He turned the phone camera and showed me... showed me Papa. And then someone took the phone away, and the call ended, and I couldn't... I couldn't..."

"Mom." Gaurav's voice was thick with unshed tears. "Mom, please."

"But it can't be true!" The words exploded from her, fierce and desperate. "Your father is there with him. Your dad promised me he'd take care of your grandfather, while I was here for my surgery. He promised! My father is strong. He does yoga every morning at 5 AM. He walks three miles every evening. He can't just... he wouldn't just leave without saying goodbye!"

The math of it didn't add up in her grief -stricken mind. How could someone be alive at midnight, laughing about mangoes and monsoons, and then simply... not? How could the universe be so cruel as to steal away the one person who had never, ever let her down? Her children stayed with her through the rest of that endless night, taking turns holding her as she drifted in and out of a medicated sleep. Each time she woke, she saw their drawn faces, their red -rimmed eyes, and knew, somewhere in the part of her mind that wasn't screaming in denial, that her midnight terror had been no dream.

When morning finally came, pale and unwelcome through the curtains, Shona rose like a sleepwalker. Her feet carried her to the living room where Gaurav sat hunched over his phone, dark circles under his eyes, testament to his vigil.

"Did you take your fever medicine?" she asked, her voice strange and distant even to her own ears. "You were burning up in my dream. You were the one who told me about..."

She couldn't finish the sentence. Gaurav stood slowly, crossing to her with measured steps as if approaching a wounded animal. When he reached her, he took her face gently between his hands, forcing her to meet his gaze.

"Mom," he said, his voice breaking on the single syllable. "Grandfather is gone. It happened last night, just after midnight. Dad called. He's been trying to protect you, to give you time, but Mom... we have to go. The funeral... we have to go to India." The slap came before Shona even realized she'd raised her hand. The crack of it echoed through the room, leaving a bright red mark on Gaurav's cheek. But he didn't step back, didn't even flinch. He just stood there, tears finally spilling over, as his mother raged against the truth.

"You're lying! The fever has made you delirious! My father would never leave me. He promised! When I was seven and scared of the dark, he promised he'd always be there. When I got married and moved away, he promised. When I had you, when I had Gauri, he promised! He doesn't break promises!"

Her legs gave out then, and she crumpled to the carpet like a marionette with cut strings. The impact barely registered. Nothing registered except the yawning chasm opening in her chest, threatening to swallow her whole. Through the haze of grief, she heard Gaurav on the phone with his father, heard the words "complete denial" and "medical emergency" and "yes, we'll be ready." She felt hands lifting her, felt Gauri's tears wet against her neck, but it all seemed to be happening to someone else, someone far away. When her sister, Geet arrived that afternoon, Shona saw her own devastation reflected in her sibling's face. They sat together in silence, two daughters orphaned by a loss too profound for words. Neither spoke of their father. To speak of him would be to acknowledge he was gone, and neither was ready for that finality.

The flight to India passed in a blur of medications and fitful sleep. Shona kept reaching for her phone, muscle memory insisting she needed to call her father, to tell him she was coming home. Each time reality crashed back, it was like learning of his death anew. The taxi from the airport moved through familiar streets that seemed foreign now, everything changed by the lens of loss. When they pulled up to her parents' house -her mother's house now, her traitorous mind whispered fears she didn't want to believe -Shona couldn't move. The house looked the same, white -washed walls and blue shutters, her father's garden spilling over with bougainvillea and jasmine. But his scooter wasn't in its usual spot. His sandals weren't by the door.

Vicky, her husband, had to practically carry her inside, where a sea of relatives waited with pitying eyes and platitudes she couldn't bear to hear. But it was her mother who broke her completely - her strong and composed stoic mother who collapsed in her daughters' arms, sobbing apologies for not being able to save the man they all loved beyond measure.

"I tried," her mother wept, her tiny frame shaking with the force of her grief. "The doctors tried. But his heart... it happened so fast, baby. He called your names at the end. Both of you. Always his precious girls." Shona tore away from the embrace, stumbling through the house like a woman possessed. Her father's study still smelled of his cigarettes, the ones he swore he'd quit. His reading glasses lay folded on his desk next to a half -completed crossword puzzle. Yesterday's newspaper. Yesterday's tea cup. Yesterday's father, who would never see today.

She found herself in his bedroom, staring at the bed where he'd slept for forty years, where he'd told her bedtime stories and checked for monsters, where he'd sat up with her through chicken pox and heartbreak and the darkest nights of her soul. The sheets had been changed, she realized with a surge of irrational anger. Who had dared to erase these last traces of him?

"He's not gone," she said to the empty room, to Vicky hovering in the doorway, to the universe that had betrayed her so completely. "He's just... he must be at the temple. Or walking in the park. He'll be back for dinner. He never misses dinner." But dinner came and went, and her father's chair remained empty. The next day brought rituals she moved through like an automaton - the cremation, the prayers, the scattering of ashes in the Ganga river that he'd loved. She performed each rite with her sister, her hands steady even as her mind screamed in protest. This couldn't be her father reduced to ashes in a brass urn. Her father was larger than life, louder than thunder, warmer than summer sun.

Back in Canada, the dream continued to haunt her. Every night at 2:47 AM, she would wake with his name on her lips, reaching for her phone to call him before remembering. This emotion was always the worst part -that crushing moment when dream dissolved into reality, when hope crumbled into truth. Months passed in this terrible pattern. Gaurav and Gauri learned to have warm milk ready at 2:30, to sit with her through the storm that always came. Vicky flew back and forth from India, trying to manage both his grieving wife and his grieving mother-in-law. Support groups were tried and abandoned. Therapy sessions blurred together. Medications were adjusted and readjusted. But grief, Shona learned, had its own timeline. It couldn't be rushed or medicated away. It had to be felt, fully and completely, before it would begin to ease its stranglehold on her heart.

The first night she woke without screaming was eight months after his death. The dream had come, as always - the video call, the still form, the white kurta. But this time, instead of panicking, she found herself studying his face in the dream, memorizing the lines around his eyes, the way his grey hair fell across his forehead. When she woke, she didn't call out. She pressed her hand to her heart and whispered, "I love you too, Papa."

A year after that midnight revelation, Shona still woke at 2:47 AM more often than not. The dream still came, though less frequently. But now, instead of denial, she met it with acceptance. Instead of screaming, she sent love across the dimensions that separated them, believing - needing to believe - that somewhere, somehow, he received it. She learned to live with the hollow space his absence had carved in her chest. She returned to work, laughed at Gaurav's terrible jokes, helped Gauri with her college applications. She called her mother every day, their shared loss a bridge across the miles. She even planted a mango tree in her home backyard, though everyone said it would never survive the winters.

But sometimes, in the peculiar darkness before dawn, when the dream felt more real than waking, she allowed herself to believe that it had all been a terrible mistake. That somewhere in India, her father was waking for his 5 AM yoga, was brewing his too - strong tea, was thinking of calling his daughters in Canada where it would still be evening, a perfect time to chat. Now, she was just a daughter, whose father loved her more than the moon and stars, whose father kept every promise except the one that mattered most - the promise to always be there. The midnight dream would probably never fully release its hold on her. But maybe that was okay. Maybe some losses were too profound to ever fully heal. Maybe some loves were too deep to ever truly end. And maybe, just maybe, in dreams at least, no one ever really had to say goodbye.

"She laughs, she breaks, she heals - and she lives beyond the Red Wine Gossips."

"Not Sure"

I'VE ALWAYS BEEN THE SIMPLE ONE.

THAT'S NOT ME PUTTING MYSELF DOWN, IT'S JUST the truth. My sister, Emma, was the spark bright, reckless, and magnetic. People looked at her the way moths look at flame, knowing it might burn but unable to turn away. I was the steady shadow beside her, the quiet one, the reliable one. And maybe I liked it that way.

Except for him.

Daniel.

The first time Emma brought him home, I felt something shift inside me. I remember the exact stupid detail he set his coffee down on the wrong coaster. I scolded him gently, and he smiled like he'd just discovered some secret about me. That smile, crooked, careless, and aimed right into me was when I knew I was doomed. But Emma got to him first, of course. Emma always got to everything first.

So I did what I've always done. I folded the feeling up like a note you're not supposed to pass, tucked it into the corners of my heart, and pretended it wasn't there. Pretended when we were all watching movies together that my eyes weren't tracking the way his hand rested over Emma's. Pretended that when he laughed, I wasn't memorizing the shape of it. Pretended that when his gaze lingered on me if it ever did, was by accident.

Years pass quickly when you're hiding.

Until the night of Emma's birthday party. The living room was packed, everyone shouting to be heard over the music. I don't usually drink, but Emma shoved a glass into my hand and teased me until I took sip after sip. The world blurred at the edges. I remember Daniel laughing at something someone said, and the sound hooked right into me. I remember leaning against the kitchen counter, pretending to be fine while the room tilted like a carnival ride.

And then he found me.

"You okay?" His voice cut through the noise, low and careful.

"Fine," I lied. My tongue felt too big in my mouth, and the word cracked in the middle.

He stepped closer, close enough that I caught his cologne, close enough that I could see the tiny scar just under his lip. My heart stuttered, a broken winged bird. And before I could stop myself before I could think I leaned forward and kissed him. It wasn't soft. It wasn't sweet. It was clumsy, messy, soaked in years of wanting and too much wine. The moment my lips touched his, shame slammed into me. I jerked back, horrified at myself. But then, oh God-his hand caught the back of my neck, and he kissed me back.

Heat seared straight through me. His lips were urgent, almost desperate, like he'd been waiting for this just as long as I had. I clutched his shirt, felt the hard press of his chest, the slide of his hand into my hair. The whole room spun away until it was only him, only this forbidden moment we'd built toward in silence. And then I broke away, gasping, trembling, and unable to look him in the eye. My whole body shook.

What had I done?

The next morning, my head pounded like a drum, and my mouth was dry as chalk. I swore to myself it meant nothing. It had to mean nothing. Emma could never know. Daniel would surely pretend it hadn't happened. I could bury it the way I'd buried everything else. So when I stumbled into the kitchen, hair tangled, stomach sick, I almost screamed. He was there.

Daniel. At the stove, flipping pancakes like this was his place, his kitchen, like he belonged here with me.

"Morning," he said, smiling that crooked smile.My jaw nearly hit the floor. "What... what are you doing here?"

"Making you breakfast." His tone was easy, casual, like this was normal. "Figured you'd need it."

Before I could form words, he crossed the space, pressed his lips against my forehead, and whispered, "Good morning, beautiful."

My entire body went rigid. "Daniel-what the hell are you doing?"

"What does it look like?" He set the spatula down and leaned on the counter, watching me. Calm.

"I'm taking care of you."

My breath came sharp, uneven. "We were drunk. It didn't mean anything. You're with my sister." His gaze didn't waver. "You think I kissed you back because of the alcohol?" I froze. My chest tightened so painfully I thought I might cry. He stepped closer. "I've loved you for years. Do you really think I haven't noticed the way you look at me? The way you shut yourself off around me?" His smile softened, almost sad. "Emma was... easy. She was there, she wanted me, and I let myself fall into it. But it's never been her. It's you. Always you." I felt the ground tilt beneath me. "No. Don't say that.

Don't, you can't." But his hand found mine on the table. Warm. Steady. Dangerous. "I'm not sure when it started," he whispered. "But it's been you all along."

I should have told him to stop.

I should have shoved him away in that kitchen and told him to go back to my sister, told him to forget the kiss, forget the breakfast, and forget me.

But I didn't.

Instead, when he leaned down and brushed his lips against mine again slow this time, deliberate-I let him. And when he whispered, "She's gone for the weekend. Just us," I didn't argue.

I told myself I would. I told myself this was the moment to pull away. But my body betrayed me. My heart had been waiting too long, and now that it had what it wanted, it clung with greedy hands. That weekend became a blur of him. Daniel's laugh spilling into my room, his shirts thrown carelessly across my floor, the way he traced circles on my skin like he was memorizing me. Every time he touched me, it felt like something inside me lit up, something I'd been starving for. But every time I closed my eyes, guilt rushed in behind the warmth.

Because I could hear Emma's voice in the back of my mind, bright and careless, telling me how much she loved him. And in the middle of his kisses, in the middle of his hands pulling me closer, my sister's face would flash in my head and I'd feel sick. I kept waiting for him to stop, to pull away, to admit this was wrong. But he never did. One night, wrapped up in the sheets that still smelled like him, I whispered, "Do you think about her?" He didn't flinch. Didn't hesitate. "No." I wanted to believe him. God, I wanted to. But something in the way he said it so fast made me wonder if he was lying. And yet, the very next moment, when he pressed his forehead against mine and whispered, *"I love you. Not her. You,"* my doubts vanished like smoke.

I let myself believe.

We stole moments in the quiet of the house-me perched on the kitchen counter, his lips tasting like coffee; him pulling me into the hallway, kissing me so hard my head spun. Every secret touch was fire and fear tangled together. From the outside, it might have looked beautiful, intoxicating, two people finally giving in to the love they'd buried. But if you looked closer, if you stepped into the silence between our kisses, you would've seen it: the tremor in my hands, the way I jumped every time my phone buzzed, the constant thrum of panic under my skin. Because no matter how much I wanted him, no matter how much he swore he wanted me, there was always Emma.

Always Emma.

And that thought I couldn't silence, the thought I couldn't admit even to myself was this: if he could do this to her, what was to stop him from one day doing the same to me? But it ended the way it always had to. Not with a scream, not with a slammed door. With a lie unravelling itself in front of me. It was Sunday night. Daniel had just left, brushing a kiss over my cheek before slipping out the back door. My chest still ached with the weight of him when Emma's voice came through the front door.

"Hey, I'm home!"

My blood froze.

She dropped her bag by the couch, humming, her phone pressed to her ear. I stood in the hallway, hidden in the shadow, trying to catch my breath.

"Yeah, babe," she said into the phone, laughter bubbling out of her. "I missed you too. I can't wait to see you tomorrow."

Her words twisted around me like a noose. *Babe.* I staggered back against the wall, pressing a hand to my mouth. She was talking to him. To Daniel. The same Daniel who had just left my bed, whose scent was still clinging to my sheets, who only hours ago whispered that I was the only one. The floor seemed to tilt under me. The next day I asked him.

"Did you break up with her?" My voice cracked like thin glass. He didn't look guilty. Didn't even look surprised. He just sighed, raking a hand through his hair.

"Not yet."

"Not yet?" My chest tightened. "Daniel"

"It's complicated," he cut me off. "You don't understand. She depends on me. She -she's not like you. I can't just..." "God." I pressed my palms to my eyes, seeing spots. "So what are we, then? Your side project? Your distraction until you figure things out?" "No," he said firmly, stepping toward me. His hands closed around mine, too warm, too steady. "Don't think like that. I love you. I do. I just need time."

Time.

That word rattled in my skull, hollow and heavy. And for the first time since that drunken kiss, I felt it clearly, the doubt I'd been swallowing down.

If he could lie to Emma so easily, why wouldn't he lie to me? That night, Emma came into my room, flopping down on my bed like she always used to when we were younger.

"Do you ever get this feeling," she asked, staring at the ceiling, "like you're not sure if the person you're with really loves you?"

The breath left my body. I stared at her, heart hammering so hard it hurt. "Sometimes," I whispered. She laughed softly, covering her face with her hands. "God, listen to me. I sound pathetic. But I can't shake it with Daniel. One second he's perfect, the next he's so far away. I'm not sure what we even are anymore."

Not sure.

The words echoed in the air between us. And I lay there besides her, listening to my sister confess the very thing I'd been trying not to admit to myself that Daniel wasn't steady ground. He was shifting sand, pulling both of us under. The days after Emma's confession were unbearable. I'd lie awake at night, Daniel's words and Emma's words tangling into one heavy knot in my chest,

I love you. I'm not sure he loves me.

Both truths couldn't exist. Someone was lying. And deep down, I already knew who. I decided I would end it. I couldn't keep stealing moments, couldn't keep swallowing the guilt every time I saw my sister smile. I would tell Daniel we were done, and maybe it would hurt like hell, but at least I could live with myself again. When he came over that night, slipping in through the back like he always did, I didn't let him kiss me.

"We can't do this anymore," I said, voice flat.

He blinked, surprised. "What are you talking about?"

"You and Emma are still together. You haven't ended it. And I can't keep lying to her face. I won't."

He frowned, stepping closer. "She doesn't matter."

My stomach twisted. "She's my sister. Of course she matters."

"No," he said sharply, eyes catching mine with a force that made my throat dry. "She doesn't. Not the way you think."

Something about his tone set my nerves on fire. "What are you talking about?"

He hesitated, then laughed softly, shaking his head like I was missing some obvious joke. "You really don't know, do you?"

My pulse quickened. "Know what?"

The sound of the front door opening cut through his words. Emma's voice floated down the hallway.

"Daniel? You here?"

I froze.

And then Emma appeared in the doorway, arms crossed, eyes flicking between us.

"Guess it's time," Daniel murmured under his breath.

The world slowed.

Emma's face didn't crumble the way I expected. She didn't look shocked or betrayed. She looked... calm. Almost amused.

"You told her?" she asked him, tilting her head.

My chest caved in. "Told me what?"

Daniel's hand brushed my arm, steadying, controlling. "That we knew."

I stared at him, then at her. "Knew... what?"

Emma's smile spread, sharp and cold. "That you were in love with him. We've known for years."

The air vanished from the room.

My knees buckled, and I stumbled back a step. "You what?"

Daniel's voice was soft, almost kind. "We just wanted to see what you'd do. How far you'd go. And you proved us right." The walls seemed to close in. My ears roared with the sound of my pulse.

"You played me?" The words tore out of me, ragged and small.

Emma's laugh rang out, cruel and bright. "God, you should see your face. You really thought he loved you? That he'd choose you over me?" She glanced at Daniel like they were sharing some private joke. "We wanted to see how long it would take before you cracked."

I couldn't breathe.

Daniel stepped closer, his eyes locking on mine, still so gentle it made me sick. "Don't take it so hard. You were... beautiful in your desperation. But that's all it ever was."

My vision blurred. The room spun. I thought I might throw up. Emma's hand slipped into his, fingers lacing like they'd never stopped belonging there. "Come on, babe," she said, tugging him toward the door. "She's had enough." I wanted to scream. I wanted to claw at them, to tear the smugness off their faces, to demand why. But no sound came out. I just stood there, hollow, as they walked away together, leaving me in the wreckage of my own hope. Later, in the silence of my room, I lay on the bed that still smelled faintly of him. My body shook with sobs I couldn't contain. The worst part wasn't the betrayal. It wasn't even the cruelty of their game. It was that, for one brief moment, I had believed him.

I had believed I was chosen.

I stared at the ceiling, my chest raw, and my mind buzzing with Emma's words: *I'm not sure what we even are anymore.*

Not sure.

The phrase curled around me like smoke, suffocating and bitter. I wasn't sure of anything anymore except this,

I would never be simple again.

"She laughs, she breaks, she heals - and she lives beyond the Red Wine Gossips."

LIFE'S SECOND SUNRISE

My Curly Hair

THE WATER WAS WARM AGAINST MY SKIN THAT February morning, steam rising in gentle swirls around me. My fingers moved through my hair, working the shampoo into a lather, when they stopped. There, on the right side of my breast, was something that shouldn't be there. A small, firm presence under my fingertips. My heart skipped, but I told myself it was nothing. Just tired tissue, maybe a cyst. These things happen to women all the time.

For weeks, I carried this secret companion with me. Every morning in the shower, my hand would find it again, and each time I'd make a mental note to call the doctor. But as soon as I stepped out, towelled off, and faced the day, the urgency would fade like the steam on the bathroom mirror. Life has a way of drowning out our whispers of worry with its constant demands. Work deadlines, family dinners, phone calls with friends-they all seemed more immediate than this small, silent thing that had taken residence in my body.

Six weeks passed in this strange dance of knowing and not knowing, of touching and forgetting.

On May 17, 2023, I finally sat in Dr. Sharma's office, fluorescent lights humming overhead. His fingers were clinical, professional, as they examined what I had been privately mapping for weeks. His face remained neutral - doctors are trained in this art of revealing nothing - but I saw something shift in his eyes.

"We'll need to run some tests, Ritu," he said, his voice carefully modulated. "It could be a benign lump, could be related to tuberculosis, or..." he paused, meeting my eyes, "it could be cancer. We won't know until we investigate."

The word hung in the air between us. Cancer, Even hearing it as a possibility felt like a door opening to a room I never wanted to enter.

May 26th arrived with the peculiar brightness that important days often bring. The hospital smelled of disinfectant and hope - an odd combination that would become as familiar to me as my own perfume. The ultrasound technician's face was too careful, too studied. Then came the mammography, the way they positioned my body like I was a delicate sculpture they were afraid to break. Blood tests, needles finding veins, vials filling with the deep red truth of what I was.

The biopsy was the worst - not the pain, but the waiting. They take a piece of you and send it away to be examined, judged, categorized. You're left incomplete, waiting for strangers in lab coats to tell you your fate.

During those long hospital hours, I discovered that Bengali dance shows could make me forget where I was. My feet would tap under the thin hospital blanket, my shoulders would move slightly to "Hawa ke Saath Saath."(an Indian song) The nurses thought I was delirious. I was just trying to stay alive in my own way, to remind my body it still knew joy, even here, even now.

The PET scan machine was like entering a spaceship - all white curves and mechanical humming. They inject you with radioactive glucose, and cancer cells, hungry little monsters that they are, gobble it up and glow. I lay there thinking about how my body had become a constellation, wondering which stars were dangerous.

The day of diagnosis, I was sitting by the window, watching life continue outside - people hurrying to work, children playing in the park across the street, an old couple sharing tea at the corner shop. Dr. Khanna entered with his team, a small army in white coats. He didn't waste words.

"It's cancer, Ritu. Stage 2. We'll need to do surgery, followed by chemotherapy."

The words hit me like physical things. I felt tears escape before I could stop them, hot trails down my cheeks. But as that first tear fell, something strange happened. I stood up, faced my reflection in the window, and saw not a Victim but a warrior.

"Ritu," I told myself firmly, "this is not the time to cry. This is the time to fight."

The calls I made were quick, efficient. Second opinion. Treatment options. Insurance paperwork. My sister Poonam arrived within an hour, her eyes already red -rimmed - she'd known before I called. My brother Sachin came straight from his office, still in his business suit, looking lost. They found me not crumpled in bed but sitting cross -legged on the floor, making lists.

"Have you lost your mind?" Poonam asked, her voice shaking. "How can you be so calm?"

How could I explain? That in that moment of diagnosis, alongside the fear, came an overwhelming wave of gratitude? Thank you, Universe, for letting me find it early. Thank you for Stage 2, not Stage 4. Thank you for treatments that exist, for doctors who know what to do.

They thought I was in denial. I was in a state of grace.

Months before, I had inexplicably started chanting "Radha" during my morning walks. The ancient texts say Radha removes obstacles and pain. Perhaps the universe was preparing me, giving me strength before I knew I'd need it. My mother, who had passed five years ago, always said the divine prepares us for our battles. Maybe she was preparing me too, from wherever she was.

In the days before surgery, I did something that might seem strange. I talked to my breast. I thanked it for being part of me for forty -three years. I apologized for what was about to happen. I told it stories of the life we'd lived together - the lovers it had known, the babies of friends it had comforted, the beautiful dresses it had filled. This part of me that had defined my womanhood in so many ways was about to leave, and it deserved a proper goodbye.

June 1, 2023. Surgery day. The anaesthesia countdown felt like a rocket launch in reverse. Ten, nine, eight... and then nothing. I woke up different. Not less than, but changed. A new Ritu, carved by necessity, sculpted by survival.

The gratitude practice I started then bordered on obsessive. Thank you, scalpel, for your precision. Thank you, sutures, for holding me together. Thank you, morphine, for the mercy of painlessness. Thank you, bedpan (yes, even you), for preserving my dignity when I couldn't walk. I thanked the night nurse who held my hand when the pain broke through, the cleaner who hummed while mopping, making the room feel less clinical. I thanked the walls for standing steady when I was falling apart.

We didn't tell Papa immediately. At seventy -eight, his heart wasn't what it used to be. So, I stayed in the hospital longer than necessary, using "complications" as an excuse. By day twelve post -surgery, I was doing yoga in my hospital room, much to the staff's amazement. The warrior pose felt different with my new geography, but I was still standing.

When we finally told Papa, I rehearsed it like a script. Sitting in our living room, his favourite chair, evening light gentle through the curtains. "Papa, I have something to tell you. I had cancer - had, past tense. It's been removed. I'm going to be fine."

His face crumpled for a moment, then reformed into something fierce. "You're my daughter," he said simply. "Of course you'll be fine."

"You'll still have to find a groom for me," I joked, trying to lighten the moment.

"Who'll marry a bald girl?" he shot back, and we both laughed until we cried, not sure which tears were from humour and which from fear.

Chemotherapy, Even the word sounds like poison, doesn't it? My naturopathy training screamed against it. My mentor, Dr. Ashwin, begged me to try alternative treatments. But sometimes the path forward is through the very thing we fear most.

The night before I agreed to chemo, I asked the universe for a sign. Something clear, undeniable. That evening, walking on my terrace, I looked up. There, formed by clouds and sunset light, was a perfect "V" shape, luminous against the darkening sky. V for Victory. V for Valiant. V for Very Much Alive.

July 7, 2023. First chemotherapy. The chair was unexpectedly comfortable, like a recliner in someone's den. The IV pole stood sentinel beside me. The drug - Adriamycin, they called it, though I renamed it Amrit, divine nectar - was the color of cherry juice. I watched it travel down the tube, into my vein, and imagined it as liquid light, finding every hidden cancer cell and dissolving it with love.

July 9th nearly broke me. The nausea came in waves, each one threatening to pull me under. My body felt like a stranger's - too heavy, too light, too hot, too cold, all at once. That night, I thought might be my last. I video -called Poonam and Sachin, just to see their faces, pretending my internet was bad when they asked why I looked so pale.

But morning came, as it always does, and I was still here.

My best friend Meena's birthday was July 15th. The doctor said I was too weak to go. I went anyway, dancing for three songs before having to sit down. "If this is my last birthday with you," I told her, though she didn't know what I meant, "I want you to remember me dancing."

The chemo cycles were like being trapped in a terrible carousel - every twenty -one days, another round. Each one brought its own flavour of suffering. The metallic taste that made everything taste like sucking on coins. The bone -deep exhaustion that made lifting a spoon feel like weightlifting.

The neuropathy that made my feet feel like they were walking on broken glass. Just when I'd start to feel human again, it was time for the next round.

But it was the hair that everyone noticed.

"You'll lose your hair," the oncologist said, like he was telling me the weather forecast.

"Even bald, I'll look beautiful," I responded immediately, surprising us both.

That night, I downloaded an app that showed me what I'd look like bald. I laughed until my sides hurt. I looked like a very wise egg. I showed Papa. "Now we'll be twins!" I told him, rubbing his own bald head.

Before the second chemo, when the falling started in earnest, I cut my long hair short. The night before shaving it completely, I threw myself a hair party. Just me, my mirror, and a playlist of every song I'd ever danced to. Five hours I danced, my hair flying for the last time. I kissed it, literally grabbing handfuls and kissing it like an old lover I was saying goodbye to. I thanked it for forty -three years of curls and tangles, of good hair days and bad, of compliments and styling frustrations.

The next morning, the razor felt like freedom.

My mentor's ad Vice transformed the experience: "Don't call it chemotherapy. Call it Elixir Therapy. See every drop as sacred medicine." So, I did. During each session, I visualized the drugs as golden honey, flowing through me with healing intentions. I thanked everything - the IV bag, the tube, the needle, the tape holding it in place. The gloves the nurse wore, the chair I sat in, the ceiling tiles I counted. Everything became part of my healing ritual.

Caring for my bald head became a meditation. Oil massage every morning, gentle shampoo, even conditioner for the scalp. I grew to love the feeling of wind directly on my skin, the efficiency of getting ready in the morning. When people stared, I smiled. When children asked, I told them I was becoming a butterfly and this was my cocoon stage.

Eight rounds, Eight times I sat in that chair. Eight times I watched the cherry -colored medicine drip into me. Eight times I survived.

After round four, they increased the dosage. My body rebelled completely. A week in the hospital, machines beeping, worried faces hovering. But I came back. We always came back, my body and I. We were a good team.

January 8, 2024. Final chemo session. I rang the bell they keep for patients who complete treatment. It sounded like church bells, like celebration, like the universe applauding.

But the preventive medications that followed were worse than chemo. Allergic reactions that swelled my face until I didn't recognize myself. My fingers like sausages, my feet like balloons. This was my dark night of the soul, when even gratitude felt hard to find.

I went deeper into my practice, Ho'oponopono - the Hawaiian forgiveness prayer. "I'm sorry, please forgive me, thank you, I love you." Over and over, to my body, to my cells, to everyone I'd ever harboured resentment against. I noticed that whenever I complained about someone, my allergies worsened. My body was teaching me that holding onto anger was literally toxic.

Sometimes, in the quiet hours, I missed Mama so much it was physical pain. She would have known what to do, would have made her special soup, would have rubbed my feet while telling me stories. But then I'd remember her strength, how she faced her own battles with such grace, and I'd find my spine again. Perhaps it was better she wasn't here to see me like this. It would have shattered her. Or perhaps she was here, in the strength I found when I thought I had none left.

The financial toll was a different kind of cancer. Savings evaporated like morning dew. Fixed deposits broken. Pride swallowed as I became dependent on Sachin for everything from medicines to groceries. The independent woman who'd built her own career now couldn't even remember to pay her phone bill on time.

The memory loss is perhaps the cruelest joke. I, who never forgot a birthday, now need three reminders to remember my own. Notification sounds make me anxious. The constant pinging feels like being pecked by invisible birds. Technology, which I once mastered easily, now feels like trying to read a foreign language.

I have fifteen years of solid work experience, but who would hire me now? I am who I used to be, but I'm not the same. It's like being a ghost of yourself, familiar but fundamentally altered.

But these two years taught me languages I never knew existed. The language of pain, yes, but also the language of transcendence. I wrote poetry like breathing - for friends' birthdays, for anniversaries I miraculously remembered, thank you notes to everyone from my oncologist to the woman who delivered my medicines. If I was going to leave this world (though I never truly believed I would), I wanted to leave it covered in my gratitude, drenched in my love.

Dancing became my prayer. Even when my feet were numb from neuropathy, even when my joints ached, I danced. Sometimes just my fingers would dance, or my shoulders, or just my heart. Music became my medicine. In the darkest moments, I'd put on the silliest pop songs and move until I remembered joy.

The introvert the doctors worried about, the quiet girl who kept to herself - she became a warrior. Not a loud, sword -wielding warrior, but a quiet, determined one who knew that survival sometimes looks like dancing alone in your room at 2 AM, writing a poem for a friend you haven't seen in years, or thanking your pillowcase for being soft against your bald head.

This is my story - a little crazy, definitely unconventional. I'm different from the world, overflowing with a love that doesn't always make sense, with gratitude that seems excessive. The world doesn't quite know what to do with me, and that's okay.

My hair is growing back now. Curly, like before, but with a mind of its own. Some days it's waves, some days it's spirals, some days it stands straight up like it's surprised to be here. I love it with the fierce love of someone who knows what it's like to lose something and get it back transformed.

Thank you, Universe, for this life that broke me open and let the light in. Thank you for the cancer that taught me I'm stronger than I knew. Thank you for the bald head that showed me beauty isn't hair deep. Thank you for the friends who loved me swollen and strange. Thank you for the family who caught me every time I fell. Thank you for the dance that never left my body, even when everything else did.

Thank you for teaching me that money matters, but gratitude matters more; That loving and respecting our relations is vital, but loving yourself is non -negotiable; That letting go of the past isn't giving up, it's making room for the present. And the present, this moment right now, even with all its imperfections, is absolutely perfect.

I am Ritu Khanna. I had cancer. I am bald and beautiful. I am broken and whole. I am exactly who I'm supposed to be.

My curly hair is growing back, wild and free, like my spirit that refused to be tamed by any disease. Each curl is a tiny Victory flag, waving in celebration of still being here.

And I am so very, very grateful.

Thank you. Thank you. Thank you.

"She laughs, she breaks, she heals - and she lives beyond the Red Wine Gossips."

My husband, My hero

It was the evening of October 13, 2012. I was walking under a canopy of wet maple trees on the street where I live with my husband. The streetlight beamed through the leaves, casting a patchwork of shadows that made me feel uneasy. As I reached Commercial Drive, the trees gave way to glass and concrete condominiums. Cars blared their horns through a haze of drizzle that smelled like ginger beef and exhaust. That's where the pain hit me. It felt like a punch to the stomach. Burning. Blackness. Head strike on concrete. Blood. I rolled over on my back; with shaking hands I called my dear husband, Vic. A minute later I could hear his shouts over the traffic noise as he ran down the street. Feet pounding down the sidewalk. Colours flashing in my head. I began to cry. Tears streamed down my face, carrying away some of the blood. When Vic reached me, I was holding my belly. He called our doctor, a personal friend who told him to give me painkillers. What kind of doctor would prescribe painkillers, sight unseen, to a woman lying on the sidewalk? I needed an ambulance, but that didn't matter in the end. Vic lifted me to my feet. We shuffled home like bombed -out refugees.

My condition got worse. Diarrhoea. Shit filling my pants before I reached the toilet. Time was flying - like a bird at altitude that seems parked in the clouds. Instead of calling an ambulance, we went to bed.

My daughter, Tanya, woke up at midnight to the sound my moaning. She walked into our room, and told Vic to take me to the hospital. We got into the car in the pouring rain. To the hospital. Wipers blasting back and forth. We hit a bump somewhere near Davis Street; I screamed murder. The distorted light coming through the windshield made the situation feel like a bad dream.

Vic said the Emergency department was too far. Instead he swerved into a side street, through an alley, and parked the car at a walk -in clinic, which was long closed. Vic knew his way around the city, but I started screaming again. He put the car in reverse and barrelled back onto Davis Street. The pain was explosive.

I woke up in a wheelchair with Vic at the helm. The drone of fluorescent lights and the smell of hospital disinfectant made me throw up. The vomit, which hit the shiny floor, tasted like coffee and salad.

The emergency room was short on beds, and long on kind nurses, who rushed to my bedside, slammed the curtains shut, and stripped off my dress. They plugged me into an IV, but the morphine wasn't enough. It's hell when the heavy artillery of pain medication doesn't help.

The nurses worked on me for around 20 minutes. Vic held my hand through the suffering. They took my blood pressure with the machine that squeezes your arm. I hate that. Behind the curtain in the next bed was a screaming child. Loud and terrible. A distraction. My dear Vic stood like a soldier at the foot of my bed. Tanya behind the glass doors. They knew I was in big trouble. I thought about dying just to escape the pain.

After seeing the ER doctor, who was bearded and tattooed, a young surgeon swept into the room. His white coat, like wings, was spotless. His pocket was full of pens, ready to write lifesaving notes. He was square -jawed and handsome. I looked up and smiled. Vic saw me, and gently caressed my forehead.

The emergency brought out all of Vic's great qualities. Strength. Kindness. Love. The surgeon moved his hands over my midsection. I shouted in agony. His hands were surprisingly rough, but warm and kind. For a second, I imagined my honeymoon with Vic, and how happy I was. But these were fleeting thoughts, the kind everyone has when they face death.

A kind security guard brought Tanya into the room as the surgeon left. Her eyes were red and puffy. Her mascara smeared down her face. The surgeon came back a few hours later and said that I had gallstones. All this was about my gallbladder?

Knowing the diagnosis eased my anxiety. I wasn't dying after all, and the anticlimax made Vic shed tears of joy. He didn't like seeing me this way. He signed his name on my consent form - soft and rolling - like our bed at home. I could have signed my own name, but Vic wanted to ease my pain.

Vic drove Tanya to her grandmother's house. She'd be happy there, getting all the touch and love that she needed. Funny how sickness makes you feel lonely for your family.

The ceiling of the operating theatre was white, of course. Just like everything else in the room, including my blanket, which was preheated and lovely. I looked up into the surgeon's eyes. They were blue like a tropical ocean. Deep and warm like Vic's eyes. I flashed forward into another fantasy, this time walking hand -in -hand with Vic down Garvis Street under the hanging flowers that line the road in spring and summer.

Another wave of pain moved over my body. Brutal and crushing. The surgeon held my hand as the anaesthetist squeezed medicine into my arm. For a few seconds, all my fear was erased. I was at peace, stuck in a moment of joy with the surgeon and my fantasy of dear Vic. All these years later, I wish that I could somehow replicate that moment. You know, put it in a bottle and open it whenever I want.

Everything went black.

The next thing I knew, I was in the recovery room with a dozen other patients. Pain shot through me as though I'd been eviscerated with shovel. Where was the surgeon? Where was

Vic? Was this the purgatory that I'd learned about as a child? A nurse came over and held my hand. I was still waking up. My body felt heavy - pinning me to the bed. The nurse said that my surgery was finished. My angry gallbladder was gone. But why the pain?

I drifted back to sleep, and was roused by the rough and warm hands of Vic. He lifted my gown and moved his hand over my incision, which was covered with a bandage and medical tape. I got the tingles. You know the ones...they move from your toes to your scalp, lifting up the hair on the back of your neck while dancing all over your scalp for a precious few seconds.

Suddenly, a new nurse appeared and offered me a pillow. I refused. The agony was too much. Then she guided me to the ward. I caught a glimpse of Vic, who somehow looked more handsome than I'd ever noticed before. He rose to his feet and began walking beside me.

Vic placed his hand on my head as I stared through the ceiling, through the roof, and through the clouds, where I walked with him down the path of an infinite forest. I closed my eyes to preserve the vision. Vic and I reached a creek with a deep pool. I could see small fish and smooth stones. Warm air moved through the trees, carrying the sweet smell of sap and moss. We stripped down to our underwear and jumped into the water. We locked lips and drifted a few feet with the current.

Hours later, the ER doctor came to check up on me.

'Sorry! I've never seen a case like this," he said. "Su, you had a serious blood clot in your lungs."

I looked over at Vic, who was staring at the ceiling with his eyes closed. He'd been with me for a whole day. In a weird way, I thought that maybe he was having the same daydream about me. The ER doctor slid another IV needle into my arm, which was bruised because of faulty insertions of previous IVs. Again, I fell asleep.

I woke up on day three. I was still in agony. "The other patients are praying for you," said the nurse in soft voice. In the afternoon, Vic went home to freshen up. He told the nurses to take care of me. I began to cry. My body hurt. I was stuck in the hospital thinking about my husband...the faithful one...the boring one...the great father...the great provider...the good cook.

The nurse held my hand and told me to relax, but my pain was brutal. I felt like a spoiled child. I felt needy and alone. When the nurse left, I accidentally rolled over and fell from my bed. I screamed louder than ever before.

Vic scolded the nurse when he returned. He was carrying a cup of coffee, which started dripping on the floor. He screamed for the ward doctor, who ran over and instructed the nurse to give me an Ativan under the tongue. Vic got one too. So, in about half an hour, he settled down...curled up beside me on the bed.

My pain had returned by evening. The doctor injected me with a steroid to reduce the inflammation, but the steroid made me anxious. I guess that can happen with that sort of medicine. Vic pleaded with the doctor to save my life, even though my life didn't need saving. Chaos. The doctor assured him that everything was fine.

We returned home on day four. The rain had ended. Soggy leaves were pasted to our sidewalk. Birds sang in the trees as traffic rushed on Commercial Dive. We walked through the front door and could smell our favourite lentil dish that Tanya was making. Vic held my hand as we climbed the stairs into the living room. Sunlight reflected off my piano and onto our bookcase.

I learned a few things while in hospital. First off, dire medical conditions almost always reveal the quality of relationships... for good or bad. Hard times expose our emotional frailties and strengths. They also cause trauma. After 24 years of marriage, I learned that my life with Vic was like being lost at sea in a beautiful ship. The ship keeps us out of the water, and makes us happy, even though we don't know where we'll end up.

"She laughs, she breaks, she heals - and she lives beyond the Red Wine Gossips."

Insecure Attachment

THE RUSTED IRON GATE CREAKED AS NAINA PUSHED it open, her heart pounding with the kind of excitement that only comes from returning home after years away. The familiar scent of jasmine from her mother's garden mixed with the dusty afternoon air of their small town, but Naina barely noticed. Her feet carried her swiftly across the courtyard, past the old neem tree where she'd once hidden from the world, and through the main door that still needed an extra push to open properly.

"Rinky!" she called out, her voice echoing through the modest two -bedroom house. "Finally, I'm back!"

The sudden shout jolted her younger sister from an afternoon nap. Rinky's eyes flew open, confusion giving way to pure joy as she recognized the figure standing in the doorway. "Naina di!" she squealed, launching herself off the bed and into her elder sister's arms.

They held each other tightly, two years of separation melting away in that embrace. Naina breathed in the familiar scent of her sister's coconut oil hair treatment, feeling truly home for the first time since she'd left for her Master's degree in Pune. At twenty -four, she'd accomplished what many in their conservative neighbourhood considered unnecessary for a girl -higher education at a prestigious university.

"You have to see my new collection!" Rinky pulled away, her eyes sparkling with the enthusiasm of a twenty -year -old who still found joy in simple pleasures. She dragged Naina to their shared almirah and pulled out several pieces of denim clothing. "Look at this shirt! I got it from the new mall that opened last month."

Naina held up the light blue denim shirt, admiring the delicate embroidery on the pockets. "This is gorgeous! I'm wearing this tomorrow when I will meet my friends for lunch. They won't believe."

A hand shot out and snatched the shirt from her grasp. "Enough of this western nonsense. You're getting married soon. It's time you started dressing appropriately."

Naina's blood ran cold. She turned slowly to face her mother, Lata, whose stern face showed no hint of warmth despite not seeing her daughter for two years. The words echoed in Naina's mind like thunder. *Getting married soon?*

"What?" The word came out as barely a whisper. Naina's eyes darted to her father, who sat in his usual chair by the window, his newspaper lowered, revealing an expression of genuine surprise. Even Rinky stood frozen, the joy of moments evaporated like morning dew under harsh sun.

Lata straightened her dupatta with the authority of someone who'd never been questioned. "I've decided. Your Master's degree is completed now. It's already difficult finding someone willing to marry you, Naina. We can't afford to wait longer."

The words hit Naina to the depths of her soul, '*Someone willing to marry you*', as if she were damaged goods being offered at a discount. Her father's jaw tightened, and he gave his wife a firm look, but Lata had already turned on her heel and walked out, leaving behind a silence so heavy it seemed to press down on Naina's chest.

"Di, I didn't know..." Rinky reached for her sister's hand, but Naina pulled away.

"Please, just, leave me alone for a while."

In their shared bedroom, Naina collapsed onto her childhood bed, the same one with the squeaky spring in the middle. The pillow muffled her sobs as she pounded her fists against it. "Why me? Why is it always me?" The questions tumbled out between gasps for air, each one carrying years of accumulated pain.

When the tears finally subsided, leaving her feeling hollow and drained, Naina stood and walked to the small storage room attached to their bedroom. It had a full -length mirror -a luxury her mother had deemed unnecessary for the main rooms. She closed the door behind her and sat cross -legged on the dusty floor, facing her reflection.

The girl staring back at her was everything her mother despised. Too thin, her mother said. No curves where there should be curves. Skin the color of wheat, when fair, was prized like gold. Naina traced her fingers along her reflection, seeing herself through her mother's critical eyes. The brilliant academic record, the scholarship to Pune, the job offers waiting for her, none of it mattered in this mirror that reflected only inadequacy.

Memories flooded back, each one a carefully preserved wound. She was in her twenties and was home for semester break, when her mother had cornered her father in the kitchen, not knowing Naina could hear from the next room.

"She needs to be married now, before it's too late. Look at her, who will want her if we wait? At least now we can say she's young."

Her father's voice had been gentle but firm. "Lata, she's pursuing her education. That's her permanent asset."

"Education won't give her children. Education won't keep a husband."

Then there was other day, when she was sixteen. Her hands trembled as she remembered finding the courage to tell her mother about the tuition teacher who'd touched her inappropriately. She could still feel the sting of her mother's words: "Don't make up stories, Naina. You don't have anything worth molesting."

Those words had sealed her lips forever. When her mother's cousin had cornered her in the storeroom during a family wedding when she was eighteen, his hands rough and invasive, his breath reeking of alcohol, she'd bitten her tongue until it bled rather than speak up. Who would believe the girl with nothing worth molesting?

The isolation had made her desperate for affection, for validation. Every boy who showed interest became a possibility for love, for proof that she was worth something. But they all wanted the same thing - a girl with low self -esteem was easy to use and discard. Each failed relationship carved away another piece of her already fragile sense of self, and her mother's disapproval only deepened with each mistake.

"You don't know how to keep anyone," Lata would say, comparing her endlessly to Rinky, who was everything Naina wasn't -fair, traditionally beautiful, skilled in the kitchen, demure in the ways that mattered to their mother.

Life changed course with the screech of tires on wet road. Her father's accident happened three months after her return, on an ordinary Tuesday morning when he'd left for the office as usual. The police said he died instantly. Naina liked to believe that was true, that he hadn't suffered.

Lata's grief transformed her from harsh critic to cruel dictator. Every bit of softness she'd reserved for her husband and younger daughter calcified into bitter resentment directed at Naina. As the eldest and the educated one, Naina was expected to take her father's government job, a provision for families of deceased government employees. Her dreams of civil service of becoming an IAS officer and making real change, crumbled like paper in rain.

"It's your responsibility now," her mother had said, not asked. And Naina had nodded, because what else could she do? Rinky was too young, too untrained for the harsh realities of supporting a family.

The years blurred together after that. Office, home, tending to her increasingly bitter mother, watching Rinky bloom and fall in love and marry her college boyfriend in a ceremony filled with the kind of joy Naina had stopped believing in. At twenty -two, Rinky moved to Mumbai with her husband, leaving Naina alone with their mother in the house that felt more like a prison with each passing day.

Thirty arrived like a thief, stealing the last of her youth while she wasn't looking. The marriage proposals had long since dried up. "Too old," the matchmakers said. "Too educated."

"Too difficult." Her mother's prophecy had fulfilled itself, as no one wanted to marry Naina now.

The afternoon sun cast long shadows through the bathroom window when the call came. Mrs. Sharma from next door, her voice shaky with panic: "Your mother fell. We've called the ambulance."

The hospital smelled of disinfectant and despair. Lata had broken her hip, the doctor explained. At sixty, recovery would be slow, difficult. She would need constant care.

Naina became a machine, functioning on routine and duty. Office from nine to five. Home to change her mother's clothes, bathe her, feed her, turn her to prevent bedsores. The woman who had once stood tall in her criticism now lay vulnerable, dependent on the daughter she'd deemed worthless.

But even bedridden, Lata's tongue remained sharp. Nothing Naina did was right. The food was too cold or too hot. The sponge bath too rough. The television too loud. Each complaint chipped away at Naina's reserves until she felt like a hollow shell going through motions.

The breaking point came on an ordinary Thursday. Naina was changing her mother's clothes, her movements mechanical after months of practice, when Lata's hand struck her face. The slap wasn't hard, her mother no longer had the strength for that, but it shattered something inside Naina that had been holding on by a thread.

She stood up slowly, leaving her mother half-dressed on the bed, and walked to the window. The evening sky was painted in shades of purple and orange, beautiful and indifferent to the pain in this room.

"Naina!" Lata's voice was sharp with indignation. "Come back here and dress me properly. This is shameful!"

Naina didn't move. She could hear her mother struggling, trying to cover herself with the sheet, growing increasingly distressed.

"Please, baby," the tone shifted to pleading. "I'm cold. I'm uncomfortable. Please."

Naina turned then, tears streaming down her face. She walked back to the bed and gently took her mother's weathered hands in hers. "Why, Maa? Why are you uncomfortable? Isn't this what you did to me my whole life? Made me feel exposed, inadequate, ashamed of my body?" Her voice was soft, broken. "Look at yourself now, Maa. This aging body you're so ashamed of, is this really everything? Is this what determined my worth?"

Lata's eyes, the same brown as Naina's own, filled with tears. For the first time, she really looked at her daughter -not at her body or her skin color or her unmarried status, but at the pain etched in every line of her prematurely aged face. She saw the little girl who'd run to her with scraped knees and been told to stop crying. The teenager who'd sought protection and been blamed instead. The woman who'd sacrificed everything and received only criticism in return.

"I..." Lata's voice cracked. "I thought I was preparing you for the world. My mother did the same to me. I thought... I thought if I made you stronger, if I made you expect less, you wouldn't be disappointed." The tears flowed freely now. "But I broke you instead, didn't I? My beautiful, brilliant girl, and I broke you."

She folded her hands,a gesture of her deepest apology. "Please forgive me, baby. I know I don't deserve it, but please... forgive your foolish mother."

The wall Naina had built around her heart, brick by brick over thirty years, crumbled in an instant. She pulled her mother into an embrace, feeling the fragility of the body that had given her life, the racing heartbeat that matched her own. Lata's arms came around her, tentative at first, then tighter, as if trying to make up for three decades of withheld affection.

"I love you, my daughter," Lata whispered into Naina's hair. "I've always loved you. I just didn't know how to show it without fear making me cruel."

They held each other as the evening light faded, two women finding each other across an ocean of hurt. Naina felt something shift inside her chest, a loosening of knots she'd carried so long she'd forgotten they weren't part of her. The warmth she'd craved her whole life spread through her like sunrise after the longest night.

When they finally pulled apart, Naina dressed her mother with gentle hands, and Lata touched her daughter's face with a tenderness that was foreign but not unwelcome.

"We have time," Naina said softly. "We still have time."

And for the first time in her life, she believed it. The broken pieces didn't magically fuse back together, healing would take time, perhaps the rest of their lives. But in that moment, in that small bedroom with peeling paint and evening shadows, a daughter found her mother, and a mother found her daughter. They found each other in the space between regret and forgiveness, where love, patient and persistent, had been waiting all along.

The woman who looked back at Naina from the mirror that night was still thin, still dark -skinned, still unmarried at thirty. But she was also whole in a way she'd never been before. Complete not because someone else had validated her worth, but because she'd finally received what every child deserves - a mother's love, however late it came.

Outside, the world continued with its harsh judgments and narrow definitions of worth. But inside that small house, two women were learning to be family again, one careful conversation, one gentle touch, one day at a time. The attachment that had been insecure for so long was finally finding its foundation, built not on criticism and fear, but on the radical act of choosing love despite the scars.

And that, Naina thought as she held her mother's hand while she slept, was worth more than all the perfect bodies and fair skin and marriage proposals in the world. She had found her missing piece not in a man's approval or society's acceptance, but in the simple, transformative power of a mother's embrace and three words spoken through tears: I love you.

The journey ahead would be long, the healing incomplete, but they would walk it together - two imperfect women bound by blood and, finally, by choice.

"She laughs, she breaks, she heals - and she lives beyond the Red Wine Gossips."

Triple Trouble

THE ALARM CLOCK SCREAMED AT SIX IN THE morning, but Meera Sharma was already awake, staring at the ceiling of her tiny one-bedroom apartment in Mississauga. Three months in Canada, and she still couldn't get used to the silence. Back in Delhi, by this time, the street vendors would be hollering, dogs barking, and Mrs. Gupta from next door would already be haggling with the vegetable seller loud enough to wake the entire neighbourhood. Here, there was nothing but the hum of the refrigerator and the occasional whoosh of a car passing below. "Mom, your alarm is giving me depression," groaned Arjun from his makeshift bed on the floor, a mattress that had seen better days and currently looked like a sandwich with him as the filling. "Depression? Baby, you don't know depression until you've seen Canadian grocery prices," Meera shot back, throwing a pillow at her twenty-year-old son. "Eight dollars for cauliflower! In India, the vendor would throw in free coriander and still apologize!" From the bed beside her, fifteen-year-old Priya mumbled something that sounded suspiciously like "Can we skip school today?" without even opening her eyes.

"It's Saturday, genius," Arjun muttered.

"Even better reason to skip it," Priya replied with impeccable logic that made Meera snort with laughter. This was her life now a software engineer turned housewife, turned single parent in a foreign land, turned whatever she was still figuring out. Three souls crammed into five hundred square feet of overpriced real estate, while her husband Raj held down the fort back in India, visiting whenever his IT job and the Canadian visa officers aligned in cosmic harmony.

She still remembered the day her elder son dropped the bomb. It was during a video call with Raj, two months into Arjun's first semester at the University of Toronto. "So, baby, how's medical school treating you?" Raj had asked proudly, chest puffed out even through the pixelated screen. "About that," Arjun had started, suddenly finding the ceiling fan fascinating. "Funny story, Dad. You know how engineers also help people? Like, biomedical engineers basically save lives too, right?" The silence that followed could have frozen hell and thawed it back twice over.

"Arjun Sharma,"

Meera had said in that dangerously calm voice that made both her children instinctively check for the nearest exit, "are you telling me that instead of pursuing MBBS like you begged us for three years, like we moved across the planet for, you're doing... engineering?"

"Surprise?" Arjun had offered weakly, his smile looking more like a grimace.

"I'll give you surprise," Meera had muttered, while Raj's face went through all five stages of grief in fast-forward on the laptop screen. "You forgot to mention this tiny detail for an entire term?"

"I was going to tell you! But then the first week was orientation, and the second week I was settling in, and by the third week, I figured I was in too deep and"

"And by exam time, you thought your mother had developed amnesia?" Meera had interrupted. "Baby, I remember every single chocolate you stole from your sister's Halloween candy in 2015. You think I wouldn't notice you switching from anatomy to algorithms?" Priya, ever helpful, had chimed in from the background,

"To be fair, Mom, you didn't notice when I didn't go to school for a week straight last month."

"WHAT?" That call had ended with Raj needing antacids, Arjun sleeping on his floor mattress as punishment which became permanent because Toronto rent was criminal, and Priya being forced to attend school for a whole month without negotiation.

The first time Meera went grocery shopping at Loblaws, she nearly had an existential crisis. The pristine aisles, the polite silence, the apologetic customers it was like stepping into another universe. She picked up a tomato to check its firmness, and the person next to her whispered, “Sorry,” and moved away.

“Sorry? For what?” Meera had asked, bewildered.

“Oh, sorry, I thought I was in your way.”

“But you weren’t!”

“Sorry about that too.” Meera stood there, tomato in hand, wondering if she’d entered some Canadian version of the Twilight Zone where apologies were currency and silence was golden. Where was the haggling? Where was the aunty elbowing her way to get the freshest vegetables? Where was the chaos, the life, the drama of negotiating onions down to the last rupee? She tried, once, to bargain. “Thirty dollars for this small piece of fish? In India, I could buy the whole fish, the fisherman, and his boat for this price!” The teenage cashier had looked at her with a mixture of confusion and fear, finger hovering over what Meera suspected was a panic button. “Ma’am, the price is fixed.” “Fixed? What if I buy two?” “Then... you pay sixty dollars?” Meera had left that day feeling defeated, muttering about capitalism while Priya walked several steps ahead pretending not to know her.

Winter in Canada was a beast she had underestimated. India’s winters were child’s play compared to Toronto’s negative-degree torture chamber. So she did what any sensible Indian mother would do she started slathering herself and her children with homemade desi ghee. "Mom, I smell like a walking samosa," Arjun had protested. "Good! At least you smell like culture," Meera had retorted, adding an extra dollop to his forehead for good measure. The gym incident that followed became legend. She had joined the local gym "New year, new me," she'd declared in January and walked in that first February morning, properly ghee-moisturized and ready to conquer the treadmill. A young man on the next treadmill had started sniffing the air like a confused bloodhound. An older lady had moved three machines away. The instructor, a perky blonde named Jennifer, approached her cautiously.

"Ma'am, are you okay? There's a very strong aroma."

"Oh, that's just my ghee," Meera said cheerfully.

"Your... ghe...y?"

"Ghee. G-H-E-E. Clarified butter. Very good for the skin." Jennifer's face went through several expressions before settling on one that was professionally horrified. "But the smell..." "Smell of health!" Meera proclaimed loudly, causing several people to actually leave the cardio section. She became a gym legend after that. People would clear a five-foot radius around her, which Meera considered a bonus no waiting for equipment.

Saturday nights were sacred in their little apartment. The routine was fixed, Meera would attempt a new recipe from

YouTube with varying degrees of success and then they'd all squeeze onto the single bed to watch a movie on Arjun's laptop. "Can we please watch something other than *Kabhi Khushi Kabhie Gham (a popular Indian movie)* for the forty-seventh time?" Arjun would plead. "It's a classic!" Meera would insist. "Plus, it's free on this sketchy website your sister found." "It's not sketchy, it's resourceful," Priya would argue, while closing pop-up ads that definitely weren't about movies. They watched everything from Bollywood classics to shaky Hollywood bootlegs. Meera cried at the emotional parts every single time, even though she could recite the dialogues by heart. "Mom, you know Anjali comes back, right? You've seen this movie more times than it has songs," Priya would say, handing her tissues. "It's about the journey, not the destination," Meera would sniffle. "Also, Shah Rukh Khan's (famous Indian actor) arms in that sweater deserve repeated viewing." "MOM!" both kids would groan in unison.

Her cooking journey was another kind of drama complete with explosions, plot twists, and gradual redemption. Back in India, she had house help and Raj, who was surprisingly good in the kitchen. Her expertise had extended to Maggi noodles and toast. But Canada had other plans. "Today, we're trying Pasta Arrabiata!" she'd announce on Sundays, laptop dangerously close to the stove.

"Didn't you almost burn water last week?" Arjun would ask. "That was a minor setback. This YouTube lady says it's fool proof." The smoke alarm became such a regular dinner guest that Priya named it Sharma Uncle. "Oh look, Sharma Uncle is joining us for dinner again," she'd say, climbing on a chair to fan it with a towel. Slowly, miraculously, Meera improved. Her butter chicken no longer looked radioactive. Her rotis were almost round. The weekend recipe attempts became family events Arjun reading ingredients like a surgical assistant, Priya documenting disasters for her "When Mom Almost Killed Us" album.

Meera's approach to her children's friendships bordered on intelligence agency surveillance. "Give me your friend Kevin's number," she'd demanded from Arjun. "Why? Did I do something wrong?" "No, but you might, and I want to be prepared." She had a whole contact list: Kevin (Arjun's friend who eats too much),

Jessica (Priya's friend with blue hair),

Mohammed (nice boy, potential son-in-law?),

Brad (suspicious, too many tattoos).

She'd call them at random.

"Hello, Kevin? This is Arjun's mom. Are you eating properly? You looked thin last time. Come over, I made extra dal." "Mrs. Sharma, I'm in class right now."

"Oh good, study hard. Is Arjun also in class, or is he bunking again?"

"He's... um..." "That's what I thought. Thank you, baby. Come for dinner."

Priya's friends eventually grew to love her too. "Hi Mrs. S, it's Jessica. Can you teach me that hair oil thing you mentioned?" "Of course, baby! But first tell me, is Priya actually at your house studying, or are you both at Tim Hortons again?" Eventually, both kids gave up trying to lie. It was easier to tell the truth than to deal with Detective Mom.

Through all the laughter, chaos, and burnt dinners, there was always an empty chair at their dining table. Raj's absence was a constant ache that video calls couldn't heal. "When is Papa visiting?" Priya would ask. "Next month, if the visa gods are kind," Meera would reply, the same answer she'd been giving for months. The immigration process moved at the speed of a sloth on sedatives. During their calls, Raj would join dinner from 7,000 miles away, propped up on a laptop. "That pulse looks a bit watery," he'd tease. "Your face looks a bit watery," Meera would shoot back, making the kids laugh. "I miss you," he'd say softly when the kids weren't paying attention. "I miss you too," she'd whisper back, then louder, "But I don't miss your snoring!"

Somewhere between the burned dinners and the successful ones, between Arjun's engineering classes and Priya actually attending school, something shifted. Meera began writing again small observations about immigrant life, funny anecdotes about cultural confusion, heartfelt reflections about family stretched across continents. "Mom, you should start a blog," Priya said one day after finding her notebook. "Who wants to read about a crazy Indian mother's adventures?" "Everyone," Arjun replied. "Your stories are hilarious. Remember when you tried to explain to the landlord why we needed a pressure cooker and he thought it was a bomb?" So she did. Her blog, *From Delhi to Maple Syrup*, became an unexpected hit. Her honest, humorous take on immigrant life resonated with thousands. Publishers came calling. Suddenly, the software engineer turned housewife turned single parent was **Meera Sharma, An Author.**

Fifteen years later,

Standing on stage at Roy Thomson Hall, Meera felt the weight of all those years melt into pride. "Ladies and gentlemen, please welcome bestselling author Meera Sharma, reading from her latest memoir, *Triple Trouble: A Mother's Journey Across Continents*." In the audience sat Arjun Sharma, now a biomedical engineer, next to almost Dr. Priya Sharma, in her final year of medical school, and beside them, Raj, finally visiting, finally here. "This story," Meera began, "starts with a crazy mom, her two kids, eight-dollar cauliflower, and a mattress on the floor." The audience laughed in all the right places. They gasped at the ghee gym incident. They teared up when she spoke of families stretched across continents. But the real triumph wasn't the fame or the success it was in the small things: the family movie nights on a bigger couch, Priya's friends still calling her for advice, Arjun teaching his girlfriend to make perfect round rotis, and their apartment becoming a hub for every homesick Indian student in Toronto. "In the end," Meera said, closing her book, "We learned that home isn't a place. It's wherever your people are, even if they're sprawled on a floor mattress complaining about your cooking while stealing extra helpings. It's in the chaos, the laughter, the burned dal, and yes, even in the apologies at Canadian grocery stores. We came to Canada seeking opportunity, but what we found was ourselves, slightly crazier, definitely stronger, and forever bound by our triple trouble." As applause filled the hall, Meera smiled through tears. Some things, she thought, never change and thank God for that.

"She laughs, she breaks, she heals - and she lives beyond the Red Wine Gossips."